Santa MUERTE

BOOK ONE

LUCINA STONE

STORY MERCHANT BOOKS

STORY MERCHANT BOOKS • LOS ANGELES • 2016

Santa Muerte

Copyright © 2016 by Lucina Stone. All rights reserved.

Story Merchant Books
400 S. Burnside Avenue #11B,
Los Angeles, CA 90036

http://www.storymerchantbooks.com

ISBN-13: 978-0-9969908-2-0

Facebook: Lucina Stone
Twitter: LucinaStone9123

Editor: Lisa Cerasoli
Interior: LC Books/Danielle Canfield
Cover: LC Books, www.LisaCerasoliBooks.com

A Note to the Readers

Thank you for purchasing, reading, and reviewing my debut novel. Your input matters. This is a revised version based on your feedback.

—*Lucina Stone*

For Juliana and Olivia—my beautiful daughters,
my constant inspirations.

THE

DANIELA

STORY

Santa

MUERTE

BOOK ONE

PROLOGUE

EMMA DELGADO WAS PACKING HER suitcase. It was her final night in her childhood home before moving from Mexico to the United States. Mother was not pleased with her recent choices or future plans, but they had come to an agreement. Emma would be released from her arranged marriage if she consummated with the man her mother had chosen. Why Mother would insist on Emma having sex with the guy was beyond her understanding. Perhaps her mother thought she was confused, and the one night would change her mind. Mother had been conjuring up strange requests since birth. Emma did her best to appease her, but there was no way she was getting out unscathed.

Emma no longer cared. She would get it over with and leave. It would be like ripping off a bandage or some other cliché—the sooner it was over, the better.

Emma had come out to her mother and refused the marriage last year. She was in love with Monica, her girlfriend since freshman year at Drew University. They wanted to get married, and there was nothing Mother could do about it.

The meaningless sex would allow Emma the freedom she always longed for, without her mother's guilt hanging heavily in the shadows. Mother had promised this would be the last thing she ever asked of her.

It's tradition. Your duty. What will your aunts think? This is part of our culture.

The statements rotated repeatedly on the conveyer belt of her mind. Maybe the distance—a whole different country—would free Emma, and help her move on from all these "traditions."

Emma packed the last of her belongings—Tibetan prayer beads and the amethyst necklace Mother had given her for protection. She took a long look at her room and closed the door behind her. She could hear her family outside in the large garden; they were whispering, and Emma could feel their anticipation.

This time of year, Merida was full of flowers. Lilies and gardenia and plumeria trees were in full bloom. The rainy season had ended and the air smelled sweet with the prospect of a new life within her grasp. Emma tried to focus on that as she walked outside to join the clan and meet the mystery man she had heard about since she was eight years old. Her thoughts were on Monica—who could never find out what Emma had to do to earn her freedom. Monica would never understand. Emma had given up on explaining her family dynamics and beliefs by sophomore year.

The garden was Emma's favorite place. Her family grew a variety of lush plants that created a sense of harmony and connection with nature. It was her retreat. Emma could hear the bees busy pollinating all the blossoms in a sort of organized frenzy. Usually the beauty of the garden made it difficult for her eyes to decide what to savor first, but now all she saw was him. Emma's mother greeted her and walked her over to the man, who was with three of Emma's aunts. He was tall and attractive, with all the grace and charm of a movie star. He smiled softly at Emma. If Emma had been attracted to men, he would have been it. She felt her cheeks flush when he looked at her. His eyes were amber and warm. To make this task easier, Aunt Lola handed her a glass of Xtabentun, a Mayan love potion. Emma declined it. She wouldn't need it.

"What time is your flight?" he asked. The tone of his voice was smooth and soothing, like honey on a spoon dipped in hot tea.

He smelled delectable, triggering a flood of pheromones as he moved closer. His voice made Emma weak at the knees. She cleared her throat. "Uh, it's at 7:00 a.m. tomorrow." Emma looked down at her hands. She felt her stomach flutter.

"Good. That gives us just enough time." He arched his eyebrow and stared at her. He extended his hand, and she readily took it. He escorted her to the casita. The small house was set up for their privacy. Emma's family took the hint and left them alone, retreating eagerly to the big house to chat privately and imagine their own version of what was to come.

Emma could hear her heart pound in her ears as he closed the door behind them. She had never been with a man before; never had the desire to. But something about this man provoked all manner of lust. Emma felt deeply ashamed to be unfaithful to her girlfriend. Before she met him, it was just an act to get through. It was her duty. It was to cleanse her future of familial guilt. But now, with the way he was staring at her....

Obligations are not supposed to be fun. At least, Emma had thought that was the rule up to this point.

$$\dashv\vdash$$

EMMA SAT IN ROW 37, seat F, in the 747, grateful no one was next to her. Every few minutes, she had to shift in her seat. Her body was sore; everything hurt. She didn't know whether to laugh or scream. Her world was upside down; she had spent the entire night making love to a man she would never see again.

Now, she had to face Monica. Emma decided she needed to tell her.

"Damn it, Mother!" she hissed to herself. This was exactly what her mother wanted.

DANIELA DELGADO WOKE EARLY. ONCE again, she had barely slept. Being home from college and back in her old room was emotionally staggering. The reality of her plan had hit her last night. It was the look on her mothers' faces that did it. They welcomed her home from another successful semester like they usually did— swarming her with hugs and kisses, like she was perfect. It was too much to bear.

They were always so proud. Daniela never felt that way about herself. Since high school, feelings of self-doubt, guilt, and worthlessness had plagued her. Her résumé of poor relationship choices helped those feelings develop and mature over time. Her moms, however, were both too excited to notice her vacant look or the weight lost.

"You look a little tired. But I just love this new haircut." Emma ran her fingers through Daniela's hair. "Lucky you got my rockin' cheekbones." Emma gave her a quick kiss. "The pixie really brings them out."

"Yeah, well, she got her radical, fashion-forward sense of style from me." Monica gave her a wink.

It was Mom vs. Mom. That's how it always was. Daniela was perfect. Each component of her flawlessness got divvied up every time a school break sent her back home. In their eyes, Daniela could do no wrong.

They grazed over her red eyes, a little puffy from crying. They didn't comment on her dirty T-shirt. The shadow of a bruise by her collarbone went unnoticed. Tired was an understatement—Daniela hadn't slept through the night in weeks, maybe months. She had nothing to say about school, her guy, or even the weather. She wanted to be pissed off over the constant glee, and their almost un-canny inability to see her for whom she really was. But that would have taken effort, too, and Daniela was finished.

No one noticed she was like one of those zombies on the old TV shows that walked around aimlessly, moaning, hoping to be put out of its misery. She was praying someone would just stick a knife in her head, allowing her blood and brains to ooze out slowly, pain-fully, gruesomely, until everything in her conscious mind faded to black. There would be no more thoughts, no more worries.

But no one did that. No one noticed her decay. Daniela became a master at hiding it all. These women gave birth to her, nurtured her, loved her more than themselves and each other. If they didn't notice this shit, who would? Maybe it had been going on for too long. Maybe that was the problem. These feelings had been around since her eyes turned a deep hazel green, since she was able to reason and understand that she was different.

Struggling with a constant angst and longing that was unfulfilled by achievements, men, and friends. It wasn't her past daddy issues; those had been well resolved. Her relationship with both mothers was perfect. It was nothing like her mom Emma's relationship with Grandmother. No matter what Emma did, Grandmother was always disappointed. She always had a reason to say "I told you so...."

Her moms were the opposite of Abeula Anaya. They worshipped her; slathered her with positive praise like butter, basted her with drippings of love and devotion, nurtured her with the best schools and activities. Imagine the devastation. To discover their prized turkey was empty and dried up despite all their efforts.

The image made Daniela sick to her stomach, confused, and more depressed. How could all this be happening to her? When had it gone so wrong? Why could she never feel like she fit anywhere? College was her fresh start. The chance to no longer be some weird misfit. For Daniela to finally feel comfortable...being Daniela. But it was the same.

The discomfort in her own skin led to a variety of poor decisions, especially since leaving home. Her moms were no longer there to tidy up all the little messes and mishaps. Or as her mother Monica would say, "to reframe the negative." A little term they learned in therapy to roast the bird to perfection.

Daniela was resigned in her decision. She was furious, but mostly with herself. She had spiraled again, and this time there was nothing anyone could do. Her mothers had tried to fix her situation in the past with therapy, medication, tutors. Anything Daniela asked for, they would try. Maybe that's what led her back home. What twenty-year-old girl wouldn't want her parents to save her?

But she hadn't been totally honest with them—about her suffering, about her grades, about the isolation since leaving home. About the boyfriend.

God. "Boyfriend"—what a word. He was anything but.

All that her research resulted in was a grim diagnosis. There was no way a hospital would help; they would just medicate her into a fog. Her mom Emma said she had gone through the same thing as a young woman, and it would pass. But this was different. This wasn't grandmother planting weird things in her head. It was real.

"Honey, it's 6:00 a.m. You asked me to wake you," her mom Emma whispered. "Aww...you look so beautiful when you sleep, my angel."

She had been saying that since forever. That's what Daniela's mothers expected—look beautiful, be a good girl, be perfect. It's finally over.

"Thank you, Mom," she managed to whisper. "I'll be back after my run."

She felt a wave of guilt. Her poor moms...they would miss her. There was just no way to make them understand. She would never embarrass them by deteriorating even further and allowing them to become engulfed by helplessness. This was the only way.

Emma tiptoed back to the door and gently closed it, leaving Daniela alone with her thoughts. She had to do this. The feelings choked her. She got up and filled her backpack with the necessary supplies she had stashed under the bed.

The morning was brisk. A shiver went through Daniela as she stepped outside. She loved the fall. Even though it was still dark, she knew the sun would shine soon, and the auburn and crimson leaves would decorate her vision. This would distract her a little bit, thankfully.

Daniela had left a folding stepstool on the side of the house last night. She quickly picked it up and carried it along. She wore a few layers, and the bulk was keeping her warm. She started walking toward the park three miles away.

Daniela walked faster, until her pace turned into a slow jog, slightly challenging with a stepstool in tow. The sun lit her way now. She squinted and looked up at the white sky. She felt like the rays were calling her home. For some bizarre reason this decision was starting to feel like she was finally making the right choice.

Soon it all will end.

Relief bathed her like the morning glow. She was headed toward peace and absolution—that much she knew for sure. She stopped running, took a deep breath, and closed her eyes for a minute, allowing the relief to stay with her a little longer.

Daniela continued her slow jog toward the park. She figured, correctly, that there'd be no children around at this time and she would be alone.

Her phone vibrated in her pocket as emails began to flood it. There would be no messages from friends, since she didn't have any. This was retailers and spam assaulting her inbox. She had cut off everyone when she was with him. Daniela berated herself daily for that move. Every foul name she could think of to describe the failure she had become was accurate: loser…asshole…dumb bitch…really dumb bitch.

Her thoughts went back to her mothers. They had worked so hard for her to get into Georgetown. She knew despite the scholarships, they had, sadly, taken out every possible loan to help pay for her education. She hoped they still had the life insurance policy for her. That was her prayer. Perhaps the insurance would help them manage the debt.

Her old roommate, Deborah, was accurate in her analysis of the whole thing: college was a joke. An institution built to keep the middle class poor. A worthless endeavor. Deborah had screamed that while drunk and parading in a T-shirt and undies down the halls one day. She flunked out and had a nervous breakdown not long after. Despite Deborah's state of mind at the time, she made sense. It was pointless to pursue a $350,000 piece of paper for a chance at a low-paying job. That wasn't going to be a problem for Daniela anymore.

She found a tree with a low-hanging branch, dropped her backpack onto the dew-kissed grass, and opened it. The rope with a noose at one end seemed to smile up at her. She had taken her time making it last night, after watching several videos to ensure she got it right. This would be better than pills; there was no coming back from a broken neck. She threw the rope over and pulled. The branch bent, a clear sign it would not support her weight.

Daniela pulled the rope back down and looked around. She spotted another tree and ran over. She was desperate; her heart hammered in her chest. She would strangle herself if she had to. The second tree was also a bust. The branch broke right off when she took a quick swing to test it.

She ran toward the next tree, the biggest of the bunch. How had she missed it? It was the only tree that still had all its leaves. Damn, it was stunning—the leaves were brilliant, and ruby red, every last one. It had a thick, low-hanging branch that seemed perfect.

Daniela set up her stepstool, threw the rope over, and tied the slack to the tree trunk. She pulled out her phone and looked at the time. She had to hurry.

She made the sign of the cross and got on her knees. She prayed, asking God to forgive her decision, but to understand her heart. She asked Him to watch over her mothers. Daniela stood up. The Lord knew she wasn't made for these times. She was too sensitive, and just not strong enough to cope with all the problems the world was dishing out. She felt God would forgive her choice. It was not that she was ungrateful for her life—just that she had had enough of the lying and pretending.

Daniela placed the stepstool under the gallows and stepped up. She adjusted the noose around her neck and tightened it. A sense of urgency flooded her. She hoped this would be quick. Her last thoughts were of her mother Emma's hands. Daniela wiped the tears streaming down her cheeks with identical hands, except hers were cold now and turning blue.

She took a deep breath and closed her eyes.

DANIELA FELT TRAPPED INSIDE HERSELF, like the opposite of an out-of-body experience. Everything hurt. She thought heaven was supposed to be...well, heaven. She should be floating and free? Her whole body ached, deep into her bones. She couldn't open her eyes no matter how loud her brain shouted to do so. Maybe it was true—suicides go to hell. Panic replaced pain as she struggled to move her arms. She took shallow breaths, trying to control the despair.

"Easy, boy—you've had quite a fall. Can you hear me?"

I hate this haircut.

Daniela couldn't speak. Her neck ached. She couldn't blink or move her arms. It was possible she'd just died and went to hell. Today sucked.

"I'm going to take you to my house, till you can go home on your own. Okay, boy?"

He had an accent Daniela couldn't determine. She moaned in response. She needed a hospital—if she was still alive.

"Take his arm there, Thomas, and we'll put him in the wagon," the man directed.

Daniela winced at being moved. She was placed on a hard floor. It was somehow a relief compared to the cold earth. She would enjoy this small sensation, a break of sorts, and deal with whatever was happening in a little bit. She took another shallow breath.

Damn, dangling from a noose feels a lot like being in a bad car accident— the air bag slamming into your face and forcing your head back so hard your neck wants to snap off.

She felt breathless and emotional, and ached everywhere. Hanging had been a bad choice. She should have gone with pills. Daniela wanted to berate herself further, but even thinking hurt. Fortunately, as soon as the hard floor started moving, the vibrations and noise lulled her into a deep sleep.

3

"BOY, CAN YOU GET UP? You've been asleep for a while now. You must be well by now."

Daniela was tucked into a child-sized bed. The man who rescued her stood at the end, looking at the "boy" who was taller and skinnier than his own lanky son.

"Thomas, he's waking. Bring up some water," he hollered. "Boy, do you have any kin around? I could send my son to let them know you are here."

Daniela moaned again. She could hear a voice, but couldn't make out what was being said. Her mind flickered with the recognition of words and she fought to open her eyes.

"Come on, sit up now."

The man sounded impatient. He reached over and pulled Daniela up, carefully touching a bruise on her head.

"Here, I think some whisky will do you better than water." He walked over and poured a cup. He placed it under her mouth, encouraging her to drink. "There you go. That will ease you." He touched her arms and legs in a rough way.

Daniela started coughing and turned away from him as she regained consciousness.

"You've had quite a fall, but nothing is broken. What were you doing on my land? I could have shot you."

"I was at the park—it's the town's property," Daniela answered softly, a little shocked her voice actually worked.

"The hell it is! You're on my farm. The town doesn't own it. We are just making ends meet, but paying on time." He sounded angry. "We're not going to lose this farm."

"Am I dead?" Daniela was hopeful. At least if she was dead, she wouldn't be as afraid.

"Dead? You fell from a tree. No one dies from that. You're lucky you didn't break anything." He smiled. "It must have been a hard hit to your head. I'm Roger—Roger Buckley. You're on my farm, like I said before. My son and I were tending to the cows when we saw you."

"Oh. I thought…." Daniela felt a flood of despair now. She had failed. She heard footsteps and looked over to see a younger man standing behind Roger.

"Da, here's the water." Thomas handed the cup to his father. He stared at Daniela curiously. "He's strangely dressed. What is he wearing?"

Roger answered with a shrug. He removed the blanket to take a better look at the clothes to which Thomas referred.

Daniela examined her clothes to see what was so strange about them. Basic black running pants, cross trainers, and a grey, puffy jacket.

Roger began checking the back of her jacket looking for something. He looked confused. "Your clothes are very different."

"Jesus! I tried to hang myself, for fuck's sake!" Daniela raised her scratchy voice and felt mortified. "Just let me go home. What time is it?"

She fumbled in her pocket trying to find her phone. Her fingertips brushed the edge of it, but something told her to be still. She looked up. Both men were staring at her strangely.

"I don't know who you are, but in this house we do not take the Lord's name in vain. Nor do we use that kind of crude language." Roger's voice was stern, daring her to contradict him. "I will hang you from a tree myself if you smart-mouth me again, boy."

Daniela swallowed, which was quite painful. "I'm sorry. I'll watch my mouth."

Jeez, guy, relax. She didn't know where she was or who these men were, and suddenly the potential danger of her situation alarmed her. *A girl passed out in a room with two guys, not good.* Even though it seemed they were trying to help her, they also seemed to be keeping her. Daniela started to sit up.

Roger and Thomas exchanged glances and nodded.

"You must be hungry. Daphne has cooked a hearty stew. Can I help you up?" Roger smiled and extended his hand. Thomas stood by to assist, if needed. "Easy now—you hit your head pretty hard, lad."

"I think I'm okay. Thank you. I'll call my parents and have them pick me up. What's the address here?" Daniela hoped they were not going to hold her hostage. A wave of dizziness hit her as she rose from the bed. She snatched Roger's arm to steady herself. This wasn't good.

The two men stared at each other again.

"Thomas can go tell your parents you're here in the morning," Roger said. "I asked you earlier if you had any kin nearby. It's late now for Thomas to be out." He helped her walk toward the wonderful smell. "That's it, boy. Nice and easy. One foot in front of the other. Attaboy, you got it."

Daniela's thoughts raced. She tried puzzling them all together, but the throbbing in her head kept distracting her. She couldn't muster the strength to be scared.

She reached the table and sat down. There was a bowl of stew in front of her: good, old-fashioned meat and potatoes with some carrots. Daniela was thankful it wasn't like her mom's bok choy and Swiss chard gunk. She looked around the house. These people were definitely naturalists. Most of the food was likely organic, since they had a farm. They must also be ultra-holistic or something, since there were just lanterns for light. It was so dim Daniela could barely make out the details of the room. Daniela was all for being eco-conscious, but these people were taking it very seriously.

The men sat down and bowed their heads to pray. A girl walked into the room.

Great—another female. Daniela smiled as a wave of relief traveled through her. She studied the girl carefully. She was pretty, with porcelain skin, but a timid, mousy demeanor.

Roger cleared his throat loudly.

Uh, oh. Don't stare.

The girl quickly sat down and bowed her head.

"Bless us, oh Lord, and these thy gifts, which we are about to receive from thy bounty, through Christ our Lord. Amen."

They ate silently. Daniela stole glances at the girl between bites of stew, trying to get a read on the situation. *Was she blood? Was she found hanging from a tree, too?* Daniela's thoughts started to jumble. The strangeness of having a man at the head of the dinner table threw her for a loop. Her own family was so different from this one—her mothers often chatted during meals about anything and everything. Here, it was just stifling silence. After several minutes of this tense tension, the spell was finally broken.

"What's your name, lad? Where does your family live?" Roger asked. "I know everyone in the area and had heard of no new families."

"Danny. My family lives about three miles down the hill from where you found me." Daniela took a deep breath. This guy kept calling her a boy. Maybe she would be safer if she remained ambiguous. All eyes were on her. She had a scratchy voice anyway. It was suddenly deeper following her attempt, which was advantageous now.

"That can't be right. Three miles from where we found you is a large lake, the largest in this county. I'm not sure why you feel the need to lie." Roger shook his head. "The state that we found you in was bizarre—lying by the tree, unconscious, with a rope by your side. You said you were trying to kill yourself, but never tied the rope. You can speak freely. No harm will come to you, lad."

"A lake? We live in the big house at the end of the block. I should call my moms. This is weird."

Nothing was making sense. Daniela reached into her pocket and felt for her phone. She took it out and pressed the home button, but the phone was dead. She placed it back in her pocket. *Shit.* She was pretty sure she had a solar charger in her backpack. She noticed everyone staring at her again. Taking the phone out was probably stupid. She sure didn't want that taken away, whether it was dead or not. "Please, just tell me where I am."

"I told you, Danny, you're at our farm: Buckley Farm. Our nearest neighbor is five miles away. There are no houses in the lake or near it. What was that in your hand?"

"It's my phone, but the battery is dead." Daniela looked around the room for an outlet or charging station.

"We don't have a telephone here, but our neighbor close to town does. He does charge to use the phone. We can take you there

16

in the morning." Thomas stared at Danny with a strange expression as he answered. "Da, he may be very ill indeed. What he called a phone looks like a small leather-bound book. Do you know what day it is?"

"Yes, it's Friday. Why?" Daniela answered between spoonfuls of stew. Daniela was annoyed. No neighbor for five miles was bullshit. This was Jersey, you could spit on a neighbor, they were so close. *Where am I?*

She looked over at the girl. "What's your name?"

The girl looked at her father.

Roger answered, "This is my daughter, Daphne. And you'll mind how you're staring at her."

Daniela turned and looked at Roger. "I just wanted to know her name." She looked at Daphne again and smiled. "Thank you for the stew. It's good."

This time, the girl smiled back.

"Daphne, mind yourself." Roger interrupted. "Look, lad, I can't have you googling at my daughter." Daniela was smirking as he spoke. "Best you mind your manners," he said sternly.

"Ha! You must mean 'ogle.'"

Roger made a sound with his teeth. That made everyone stop and sit up a little straighter. "I think you can stay in the barn to-night."

Daniela's smile faded.

"I'm sorry, Mr. Buckley," Daniela said into her bowl of hot food. She hoped he was joking about sleeping in the barn, like Thomas was about the book.

After dinner, Thomas handed Daniela a wool blanket. "You'll be comfortable in the barn. It's warm. I'll take you out there now."

"Seriously?"

Daniela followed him unenthusiastically. These people struck her as no-nonsense types. She'd heard rumors about folks like this, but didn't have much experience with them. When you're the only child with two moms, you pretty much get everything you want, and then some. She saved the argument, knowing she'd be wasting her breath, and trailed behind. Once outside, the darkness engulfed them. She couldn't see any lights for miles. Lots of stars though. Thousands. This might be the clearest night she'd ever seen. Thomas opened the barn door; a warm glow escaped with the scent of the animals inside.

Daniela could see a lantern hanging on a wooden post and a rickety ladder leading to a hayloft.

"Climb up these stairs and sleep above the animals. It'll feel nice and toasty up there once you get under this here blanket. I'll see you in the morning." Thomas smiled. They were the same height, after all.

Daniela was 5'9", a great height for a young woman, but short for a man. She noticed he looked young, too, now that she was alone and so close to him. "How old are you?" she asked.

"Nineteen. And you?"

"Twenty. You look don't look nineteen," she remarked. "I hate sleeping in a strange place. Can't I sleep inside?" Daniela gripped the coarse wool blanket. It lacked any inkling of comfort and smelled like feet.

"No. Not with the way you were staring at my sister. Da will never have it. Are you married? Are you running from a family, then?"

"No! God, no! I was trying to kill myself—I told you. I'll go home in the morning, but I would appreciate you not mentioning how you found me to my moms. I just need tonight to think about what to tell them."

"You have more than one mother? Are they sisters? My mother died last year. I wish that she had a sister who could be with us." Thomas rubbed his hand over his chest like it hurt him. "What's the matter? You look like you just took a swig from a sour milk jar."

"Whatever." Daniela reached out and snatched the blanket and the lantern, then headed toward the stairs, upset.

"Goodnight, then."

Thomas walked out of the barn and closed the large door behind him.

What a chooch! Sisters? Really? Daniela was appalled there were still ignorant people in the world. She reminded herself of what her mothers always said, murmuring the words to herself like a mantra.

"Not everyone is going to understand our lifestyle, but we can practice tolerance and kindness no matter what."

Bible beaters were not the most tolerant people, and these
Buckleys were truly strange and surely Bible beaters. They didn't
dare start dinner without that prayer. And the kids seemed to be
brainwashed, like they'd been coded to comply. How come Daniela
didn't know about this farm before? Her thoughts were still jum-
bled. Had they transformed the town park into a farm since she left
for college? That didn't make any sense.

She wrapped the blanket around her shoulders and listened to
the animals below. She was not an outdoorsy type, yet, oddly, she
fell asleep without much effort.

She woke from a strange dream about her mothers. When she
realized where she was and that the lantern had gone out, she sat up
vigilantly, like a dog on watch. Her heart pounded and her anxiety
returned. She looked around and listened carefully. Daniela could
hear every sound in the night—the animals stirring, the wind whis-
tling in through the crack in the barn door. She swore she could
even hear the bugs breathing and the stars shining in the sky. This
sensitivity made her feel crazy.

Daniela thought about her one and only camping trip, years ago
when Monica was a troop leader for Girl Scouts. That had ended
badly. Daniela had been too scared to sleep in the cabin and drove
her mom crazy, until Monica agreed to sleep in the car with her.
Daniela still earned her badge—her mom saw to that, even if Dan-

iela had scared the shit out of everyone with her rantings about seeing and hearing ghosts. Daniela looked around the loft again: it was way better than camping but still creepy. This fear of the dark made her feel so young again. Once she confirmed that she was, in fact, all alone, she slowly curled back into a ball and slept.

"Wake up, we're going to town," Thomas called up to Danny. "It's after six. My sister left you some oats. If you hurry, they may still be warm."

Daniela sat up and ran her fingers through her short hair. "I'm up. I have to pee. Where's the bathroom?"

"Out to the left. You can wash outside. I'll meet you inside, as soon as I square up on my morning chores." He stayed in the barn and started tending to the animals.

Daniela grabbed the blanket and made her way down the stairs. She tried to hurry, before she had an accident. She turned left once outside and saw a small shack. She shook her head, not believing that she was looking at an outhouse.

God, these hippies take things a bit too far. Composting toilets, no lights, off the grid—where are the dreadlocks, the pottery wheel, and the pot plants? Primitive.

The stench upon swinging the door open was enough to make her want to pee outside. She thought earth muffins were supposed to smell like patchouli, not total shit. She hovered carefully over the seat and held her breath. Well, her gag reflex was back.

I guess that's a good sign; no permanent damage from the noose.

She was positive she would have known about this farm. Daniela quickly ran her fingers through her hair wishing the outhouse had a mirror. She hadn't thought she would have to worry about her hair. The impulsive decision to cut off all her beautiful curls was a goodbye statement.

This all felt so strange. How was she still alive? How could they not have a phone? Where were the outlets? The indoor plumbing? She needed to check her backpack for the solar battery. This felt like a camping trip that wouldn't end. She wanted to be home, to take a hot shower and change her undies. For the first time in weeks, she was looking forward to something.

DANIELA LOOKED AROUND AS SHE walked to the house. She was amazed at how open the space felt. There was no noise from traffic, or the usual neighborhood sounds—music, doors slamming, laughing—only the sound of free-range chickens clucking around in front of the porch. She didn't see any solar panels or methane converters on the house. Despite that, the air was crisp and her lungs expanded, taking it all in. The air quality was great. It smelled like farm, yet fresh and clean. She walked up the steps of the porch and let herself in. She could smell bacon. Daniela was normally a non-swine eater, but the aroma was tantalizing. Besides, she had had that meat stew yesterday, so her attempts at veganism were shot already. Her stomach growled in anticipation. She could see Daphne by the stove, with her back turned.

"Good morning, Daphne," Daniela called out.

Daphne quickly turned and gave her a small smile. "Good morning, Mr. Danny. I have some oats for you, and some bacon.

You can sit here in the kitchen." Daphne pointed to a wooden wing-back chair.

The kitchen lacked everything but the bare basics. It had a small stove that would fit no more than two pots at a time. There was no counter space, just a white sink and small square table in the center of the room. On the other wall was a buffet and hutch with some white platters displayed—minimal, compared to her moms' commercial grade Viking and open concept kitchen. They had enough counter space to cater a party of a hundred or more.

Seeing this small kitchen put into perspective what was important; sometimes less is more. Maybe this family wanted to simplify from the opulence of modern society.

Daniela looked carefully at Daphne. In addition to the hairdo, she was dressed kind of weird. She had on a long dress with long sleeves that made her body shape appear boxy. The waist was low on the dress and Daphne was fully covered.

A vintage piece, for sure, Daniela thought. *Maybe they're Mormon?*

Usually, those women wore a solid-color dress, but Daphne's had a red-and-black checkered pattern, a white collar, and buttons down the front. Her shoes were a dull calf-brown that resembled Mary Janes, except they were pointed and had a second strap across the front. They were cute, not something Daniela had seen before, and certainly not shoes she imagined Amish people wearing. Since there are no Amish in New Jersey, she dismissed the idea immediately.

"Are you guys Pentecostal or Evangelical Christians, or perhaps some other religion?" Daniela asked while taking her seat. "It's cool if you are. I just want to make sure I'm culturally sensitive." Daniela smiled warmly at Daphne.

"Mr. Danny, sir, we are Protestant," Daphne answered as she placed a bowl of oatmeal in front of her and smiled back. "Are you feeling better, sir? Does your head still hurt you? I could make you tea."

"I could so use a latte right now. I don't imagine you guys have an espresso machine."

Daphne wore a confused expression, as if Daniela had responded in another language.

They didn't seem like latte people, Daniela realized. She didn't even see a French press. "Tea is fine, thank you."

Daphne turned and looked at Daniela, nodded, and walked over to the stove.

"Mr. Danny, sir, we've not got that expression machine, but Da has gotten us a fine radio. Would you like me to turn it on for you, sir?" Daphne walked over to the hutch and turned the knob. "I didn't have time this morning to check the paper for the radio schedule, like I normally do. Some days it's just sports. Da loves to listen to the Princeton Tigers football games. Do you listen?" Daphne looked over at Daniela and they exchanged brief eye contact.

"I'm not into college sports. I didn't even know Princeton had a team called the Tigers." Daniela continued examining the small kitchen.

"Indeed, they do. Da says Coach Roper has a great team this year. Usually, it's preaching in the morning from the St. Thomas Episcopal Church or the presidential campaign with W.H. Craw-ford." Daphne finished fussing with the knob and a voice fought through the static without much success. "Occasionally, the Hotel Commodore Orchestra is on, but my favorite program is in the evening—music from the Capitol Theater. Do you enjoy music, Mr. Danny?"

Daniela stared into her bowl of oats. It was a thick mass with a pat of butter on top. If she ate this whole thing, she would need to use the outhouse again, and soon. She didn't want to go outside. Maybe if she ate just a little, she would be home in time to use her own bathroom.

"Music, did you say?" Daniela asked between thoughts. "Yeah, sure, I'm into different genres." Daniela smiled again at Daphne. She looked pretty young, too. "Hey, do you go to Central High, or are you still in middle school?"

Daphne worked the knob to find another station. "School, sir? I learn at home with my brother."

"Well, homeschool has its advantages, for sure. How old are you?"

"Sixteen, sir," Daphne answered shyly.

26

"No shit. Wow, for a sixteen-year-old you sure do a lot of housework and cooking. That's really Montessori." Daniela took her first bite of the oats and chewed carefully. "I took a class on learning theory at school," she mumbled with her mouth full.

Daphne walked over with two bacon strips on a plate.

Roger walked into the kitchen. "How's he doing?"

"Still a bit daft and talking queerly," Daphne replied, avoiding eye contact with Danny.

Daniela reacted with a sudden jolt. "Excuse me, are you referring to me as 'daft,' as in dumb?"

"Yes," Roger answered.

"And 'queer' as in my sexual orientation, or weird?"

"I told you last night, lad, to mind your mouth in front of my daughter." Roger glared at her. She could tell he was irked. "Go on, Daphne, start your lessons."

Daphne all but ran out of the kitchen and into the living room.

"Lad, we'll take you to an asylum, there is one a few miles away. Seems you need the help. Eat, and we'll be on our way."

"No! I don't need any psychiatric help. I'm not suicidal anymore. I'm feeling better this morning. I just want to go home." As the words left her mouth, Daniela wondered if it was true. Did she feel better? She had attempted suicide the day before—was that enough to cure her of her obsession with it? Had she just needed to go through her plan and fail in order to feel better? Right now, all she wanted to do was hug her mothers. They had to be worried sick. "Please, Mr. Roger, just let me call my family and go home."

27

Roger looked carefully at Daniela. "Tell me, Danny, where is your family from? Your skin has brown coloring to it and you have fine features, almost dainty, like a girl. You speak well too, musta had some schooling."

"I'm half-Mexican and half-Italian," Daniela answered smartly. She couldn't help her neck sway as she responded. What the hell is with this guy! Even if she didn't know her father, she sure as hell knew her ethnicity. Her mother had told her that much.

"I thought you looked slightly colored," Roger responded, seemingly impressed with his own detective work.

"My God. Did you just use the word colored? What is this, 1980? What are you, Irish or something? Newsflash: no one is white anymore!" Daniela was getting pissed. In the background, she could hear the radio as the station finally came through. The man's voice sounded strange. "People are multicultural, Mr. Buckley. Elevate your consciousness."

"…Earth shocks were recorded beginning at 3:15 p.m. until 3:22 p.m. yesterday afternoon, in Washington. These shocks were recorded on the Georgetown University seismograph. Father Tondorf, the director of the observatory, said he was unable to estimate the probable distance or direction of the disturbance from Washington, but believes it may have originated in New Jersey." The announcer paused.

Daniela mumbled, "What are earth shocks? Why didn't he say more?" She continued to listen intently.

"In international news, Mussolini scoffed at his Parliament, stating he predicts a long Fascista rule, and has demanded an extension of his powers."

Daniela's heart stopped. "Wait, did he say Mussolini?"

"Yes, lad, Mussolini, the Prime Minister of Italy. Don't you listen to the news?"

The Amish outfit, the lanterns, the *racism*...no telephone, the tiny stove, the old-fashioned radio...Daniela's mind madly tallied a list of things that just don't fit. "What day is it today?"

"It's Friday, lad, just like yesterday was Thursday."

"No, no, no, no, I mean, what year is it?" Panic surged through Daniela's veins.

"Today is Friday, November 2, 1923." Roger could see the sudden distress in her face. "What day do you think it is?"

"This is fucking crazy!" Daniela yelled, pointing at Roger and Daphne, who had returned with the shouting. "You people are fucking nuts! I'm getting out of here." Daniela shoved the table forward and lunged from her chair. She slammed into Roger hands first, thinking she'd either plow through him or he'd move. He didn't budge.

"Get out of my way!" She pushed him again. Nothing. "I can get home on my own!"

She was going to have to kick him in the nuts. Damn it. She hated violence. Her resolve started to crumble as all her efforts to flee were rendered futile. "Fuckin' farmer. Move out of my way! You're crazy if you think I'm staying another second here."

"Good grief, you poor bugger. You are a loon."

Roger anticipated a knee to his nuts and blocked her kick.

"Easy, lad, you're free to go. I won't stop you, but you look as if you still need help. Now calm down, and let me take you home." Roger stepped to his left to allow Daniela to see she could leave. Her shoulders relaxed, but she was still stiff with fear.

"I think I hit my head too hard. Everything is off." Daniela started to cry.

Roger gently placed his hand on Danny's shoulder to reassure the lad that it would be all right. He'd never seen a lad who was so emotional. Irish families were a stoic bunch. Maybe the dago or spic side the boy claimed was to blame. Danny continued to cry despite Roger's attempt to soothe him. This went on for a whole half of an hour. Roger was surprised. This sort of coddling would have calmed a brand new widow by now. Roger showed Danny the date on the *Daily Record*, the newspaper Thomas picked up in the mornings. He had Danny drink the hot tea Daphne had put out for him and vowed with his right hand to God that this was neither heaven nor hell, but the Buckley Farm, on Friday, November 2, 1923. If the lad could see for himself that three miles out was just a lake, and not some kind of park with slides and swings for children, and a separate park for dogs—whatever that meant—perhaps Danny would willingly go to the asylum.

"Come, I'll walk you back to where we found you, and then you can show us where your home is." Getting Danny out of the house was a good start, Roger decided.

The crying suddenly stopped.

"That's a great idea. Yes, please, and then I'll let you meet my moms and you'll see that I don't need a psychiatrist."

Roger walked her toward the front door and out of the house.

"Yes, of course. I can't wait to meet your mothers." *Doubtful,* Roger thought. *This boy ain't got the sense of a goose.*

"YOU WERE LYING THERE, UNDER the devil's oak tree."
Roger pointed.

Daniela looked around, trying to find something, anything familiar.

"We came to check the cows after the earth shock, and there you were. I would not have brought you back to my home normally, due to superstitions about these types of trees, but I didn't think that you were evil." Roger studied Danny. "I hope I was right. Do you know about these trees, Danny?"

"No," Daniela answered. "What's an earth shock?"

Thomas laughed, then answered for his father. "The ground swaying and moving. Danny, you're hopeless."

"Shut up! You mean an earthquake?" Daniela suspected the Buckleys were not well-educated.

It's time for a new curriculum with the homeschooling, she thought. *Even I know about tectonic plates, and I fucking hate science.* "It's a beautiful tree. The leaves are magnificent. It's the only one that hasn't lost them and the branches are strong. That's why I picked it. I don't know anything about this tree, or any other oak belonging to the 'devil.'" Daniela used the sign of the horns. *Duh?*

Thomas continued to smirk.

Daniela flipped him the bird.

"Can it, you two! Neither of you know from nothing," Roger insisted.

The field looked the same to Daniela, but she could smell water ahead. She took a few steps forward, getting closer to the tree, and on higher ground too. From here, she could see that there was, in fact, a large lake. She couldn't see any houses. The park was definitely MIA. *What is going on?*

"They say these trees are portals to hell," Roger continued. "People shouldn't touch them, or they could get cursed."

"Nonsense! It's an oak tree." Daniela's patience was at its end. "Let's walk on, please." She felt the hair on her arms stand on end as she walked past the large tree. A shiver went down her spine. She didn't want to contemplate that she may have been punished somehow for trying to end her life—that she was you-know-where. The God she believed in was merciful and loving—the reason she wanted to go to heaven in the first place. *There's no way this could be heaven.*

Not only was her God merciful, but He believed in indoor plumbing. And, of course, God was a vegetarian too. And if she wasn't dead or in heaven…. Her mind felt like a scrambled egg, whisked with odd thoughts.

They continued to walk at a brisk pace. Once they reached the lake, there were still no houses in sight. Where her house was supposed to be, there was nothing but water. She thought about when the lake was drained and the houses were built. Even though it was a flood zone, they never had any water problems. Now, Daniela understood what could happen without those pumping stations. It was a ton of water the town was holding back and diverting. Was that in 1940, when they drained the lake and started building?

Her mothers' home was built in the 1990s, an old McMansion. This was crazy. She turned around and looked at everything. This really didn't look like hell either. The outhouse did, but these people had been civil, even sweet, and the oatmeal was out of this world.

Time travel? Really?

Then another notion hit her: perhaps she did need a psychiatrist. This could be a delusion of some kind, brought on by stress. She had been suicidal for a long time; maybe her mind had fully snapped. Daniela rubbed her hands through her short hair, regretting chopping it for the hundredth time. The haircut alone was reason for a psychiatric evaluation.

"Okay, let's go. I'm obviously not thinking clearly." She looked at Roger and Thomas, who seemed consumed by pity. She swallowed the lump in her throat and refused to cry. "Let me just get my stuff. I have to see someone. I'm about to spaz. This is so fucked up. Look at you two." Daniela referenced their overalls. Typical farm clothes, she guessed, but totally weird. Her words affirmed her decision to get help.

The Buckleys were staring at her like a dragon had just flown out her ass.

Her moms would be proud of her for deciding to get help, at least. "Sorry, I'm just trying to get a grip here and get back home. Again. I'm sorry for everything."

"What date do you think it is, lad?" Roger asked carefully.

"Um...." She did a quick finger count. "Saturday, November 2, 2030."

"Right." Roger looked over at Thomas, who was trying to hide a smile. "2030? That's over a hundred years in the future, lad. And throwing yourself from a tree...? You're quite unwell."

Daniela laughed. "I'm talking to people in 1923. Yes, I'm unwell. Although, if this is a delusion, it feels so real. Weird." Daniela reached into her pocket to feel for her phone. She pulled it out and looked at it. The battery had charged enough for her to use it. She was hesitant to turn it on in front of them; she had enough to deal with. "I'm gonna look around a bit more, okay?"

She walked away and pretended to look around for a five-bedroom house with a three-car garage under some leaves. Once alone, she turned her phone on. She saw she had a missed call, but there was no service in this area that had no houses, no electrical wires, and one mighty oak tree that was owned by the devil. At least the last webpages she had pulled up were still cached. Her Wi-Fi signal seemed to be working.... strange. Where would the signal be coming from? There were no fiber optic networks or Internet service providers in 1923. Maybe the devil tree was a hotspot? She started to go through her phone to determine what was working. Her signal was weak. No Bluetooth. None of her apps worked, and everything else was slower than she was used to. Her pictures, videos, and music were still intact, at least.

The men eyed her curiously from afar.

She murmured to herself quietly, keeping a watchful eye to avoid the men. Her thumbs were typing away trying to determine what else was working.

"Lad, what is that you're holding?" Roger called out. "Are you writing? Is that your notebook again?"

"Oh, hang on. I think I see something over here." Daniela gave them a wave. She could tell they were growing impatient. What was she supposed to do? Tell them, again, that it was her phone? A phone that could also be worn or used as a watch, or even better, that the phone/watch could project onto any flat surface?

That wouldn't sound crazy at all.

She couldn't risk losing her phone; her whole life was on it. She smiled, feeling normal with her phone in her hand. Having it with her and seeing it work confirmed in that moment that she wasn't crazy or dead. It was her beacon of hope. She turned and looked at the men, who were quickly approaching. Then she glanced back at her phone. The juxtaposition of them and her modern technology in this new reality of hers was discordant. The men moved closer and looked over each shoulder as she slid it out of sight.

"Danny, did you find your house?" Thomas asked with a tone of both mockery and excitement in his voice. "You're clearly nuts, but what if…?"

"Don't be daft, boy. And don't encourage him. He's not well." Roger spoke sternly, but he was also looking at Danny with blatant interest. "You can't lie anymore. There is nothing at the lake. The future boy joke is over, Danny." He swallowed audibly. "Let's go back now and see what else is in your bag. I need to make sure you don't have anything dangerous with you. Come on, boys."

THERE WERE NOT ENOUGH INTERESTING items for Roger to seriously consider any claim of time travel. The only unexplainable item was what the boy called a "phone," but once they got back, it didn't work anymore. The boy claimed its "battery ran out," as if it were an Eveready flashlight. What he called a phone looked like a piece of black glass that fit into the palm of his hand. The lad had acknowledged that the lake was real. His story about houses and parks was unbelievable. Neither Roger nor Thomas was willing to play dandies anymore to this game the lad had concocted.

"Danny, you're a colored boy. You best get back to where you came from, or there could be consequences," Roger had explained. "Now, there was an article in this morning's paper that left me uneasy. A colored boy assaulted a woman in the next town and the police are looking for him." He paused as if waiting for an admission. After a few seconds he continued. "Danny, you do not strike me as dangerous, but you're the only unexplained Negro in the area." Roger seemed to grow more annoyed with every passing second of her silence. "Now, I don't want anything more to do with you. If you don't want to go get yourself some help, then that is your choice. But if you're not gone by daybreak...." Roger showed Danny the gun in his holster. "I will remind you that I could shoot you for trespassing on my property."

"I promise to stay in the barn and not be of any further trouble, Mr. Buckley. I will be out of here in the morning."

"Before we go to market, boy, I want you gone." Roger gave Thomas a nod and they left.

Once alone in the barn, Daniela took an inventory of everything she had in her possession. She had no money or plan. Worse, she was "colored" in a time when it was not cool. There weren't any civil rights yet. No Dr. King or Cesar Chavez advocating for basic human decency. She had thought she was just dealing with a family of off-grid hippies. This was way worse; a time-traveling colored boy! Surviving was going to be hard, never mind getting back home.

She looked down at her tan hands. It was hard to believe a simple shade would make such a big difference. Last night, she had shared a dinner with the family; now, she was out in the barn like a dog no one wanted. Roger even thought she might have hurt a lady in town, even though he, himself, found her unconscious on his property. She had to get back home, and fast. There was only danger for her in 1923.

Daniela wondered how her mom, Emma, would handle her current predicament. Mom had military experience and knew about being in enemy territory. She had been wounded in Iraq and was lucky to be alive. Although badly injured, she had managed to save lives. Mom always said that it wasn't the wounds that killed a person—it was the fear.

Man, if only I took after my father this one time. Even though I never met the guy, at least he was white.

Daniela hated to think about her father, or as her mothers referred to him, The Donor. Emma knew nothing about him; all she could tell Daniela was that he looked like a movie star. Daniela had spent most of her childhood pretending every handsome male actor was her father. The only thing he gave her was curly, often frizzy, hair. Maybe he was a dark Italian or something. Daniela knew she resembled Emma in skin tone and features. There was no way she could "pass," no matter what her father's ethnicity was.

"Father"—what a word. He was anything but.

Daniela shook off those thoughts. She needed to stay focused on her situation. The Buckley farm would certainly qualify as hostile territory. The only items of value were her gold chains. She imagined selling them might get her enough to survive until she could get back home. One of her chains had an amethyst charm that her grandmother had given her. Her family wore the gemstone in the same way—a large rock, carved and polished, set in gold on an eighteen-inch gold chain. The back of the stone was marked with an inscription Daniela did not understand. This was a priceless piece she could never part with. The other two pieces of jewelry would need to go. The shitty chain with a heart Jack gave her was garbage; she wouldn't get much for it, but it was a start.

Daniela was filled with regret. How could she have been so stupid? She took some deep breaths and tried to center herself. Being scared shitless was going to amount to mistakes. She had to focus on the here and now.

If Mom could make it out of the Middle East, then I can make it out of here. Bravery was somewhere within her.

The sound of crying got Daniela's attention and forced her out of her misery. She looked out the small window in the barn loft. Daphne was running from the house to the chicken coop. Roger exited the house and walked toward the field, ignoring Daphne. Positive that Roger was gone, curiosity got the best of Daniela. She went to see what was going on. Daphne was such a mousy girl, this much emotion must have meant something big. Talking to white girls was a sure way to get shot, but Daniela could still hear her sobbing and felt badly for the kid. With Roger gone, maybe the girl could give her some info on a safe place to go.

Daniela made her way around to the coop and saw Daphne sitting on the ground wiping away tears. "Hey there. Are you okay?"

Daniela watched curiously as the timid girl seemed to transform without her father around.

"Yes, it's just my da. He gets mad and hits me." She wiped her eyes with the sleeve of her dress. Daniela noticed there were buttons missing from the front.

"Jesus, what a caveman. Where did he hit you?" Daniela leaned down to inspect Daphne for bruises. "You're sixteen. Way too old for a spanking. What's his problem?"

Daphne shuffled back a bit, pressing herself against the wall. She was scared. The expression on her face was one Daniela knew well. Jack had been hitting her at school, and she never told anyone. She was always too afraid to press charges—too embarrassed also. Daphne had a large contusion on her wrist, and a swollen cheek with a visible handprint.

"You need some ice or something cold for your cheek, Daphne." Daniela was disgusted with Roger, and with herself. Memories assaulted her. The more she looked at Daphne, the more she felt as if she was staring into her own soul.

"No, it's okay. Thank you, Mr. Danny, sir. Please don't tell my da." She looked up with a pleading expression. "He won't be pleased with me talking to you."

Daniela got the hint. He didn't want her talking to any boys. "Is that why he hit you? Was it for talking to me this morning?"

"No, sir. I asked about you when Da returned. He got awful mad and hit me. Said I had no business asking after you." Daphne looked around to make sure they were still alone. "Da and Thomas are preparing the milk and other goods to take to the market tomorrow. They are in the back barn, so we can talk for a bit. Is it true you're leaving in the morning?"

"Yes, but I don't know where. I'm pretty open to suggestions, if you have any." Daphne's comments about her father had left an

42

uneasy feeling in Daniela's stomach. Jack got like that when he was jealous.

"Can I go with you?" Daphne asked. "I won't be any trouble. I could look after you, and…."

The question washed over Daniela like a bucket of cold water.

"Is your dad doing more than just hitting you?" Daniela didn't want to know the answer. The question just fell out. Instinct. Fear. She cursed herself. She wasn't a professional counselor. There was nothing she could do for the girl. The look on Daphne's face was enough to confirm her suspicions. "Shit. Don't tell me."

Daniela let out a long sigh. *Some things you can't un-hear. Shit….* It's what her mom always said about knowing the full story, understanding the truth behind any given situation; you become a part of it. The voice was echoing in her head. *"Do something, Daniela. Help her."*

"Kelly, at the other farm, has two kids by her da. I don't want to end up like that. He won't stop, and it gets worse every time. Please!" Daphne grabbed Daniela's arm. "I don't want him to, but he doesn't listen and beats me. I've been able to get away, but I don't know for how much longer." Daphne loosened her grip as if the confession relieved her some.

"I can't just take you, Daphne. I don't have any money or anywhere to go. Your dad saved my life. I can't just steal you away. What if he calls the police and—" Daniela was outraged by the idea that Roger could abuse his own daughter like this. Roger had just played the "concerned citizen" for a woman in the next town. Meanwhile—this? *What a scumbag.*

Daphne pressed her hand to Daniela's mouth. Her eyes seemed to sparkle with hope, as if she knew Danny was playing the role of the logical, reasonable runaway, but was going to take her along in the end.... "I know where we can go. I have some money. He won't find us in New York City. Maybe we can get married or something, and then he can't take me away."

"Whoa—no way! Listen, you trusted me with your secret. Now, let me tell you mine." Daniela pulled her shirt down in the front to show Daphne that she had breasts. "I'm not a boy. I'm not going to be able to protect you the way you're thinking. Your dad also said I'm colored and—"

"I know you're not a boy. I figured it out this morning, with all the crying." Daphne arched her eyebrow.

Daniela had seen that arch before. Monica used to do that when Daniela was small and had fits about bedtime.

"Believe me, if I would have told, there's no telling what my da would have done to you." Daphne took a breath, and seemed to shake away the thought.

Daniela was filled with doubt. She wasn't strong like Daphne now seemed to be, and was still trying to figure out how to act brave. Daphne was ready to up and leave her abuser, her whole family. Now. It had taken pamphlets and months of secret meetings with a professional for Daniela to even begin to understand what this girl seems to intrinsically get.

"Look—my da was a good man, but since coming back from the war and Ma dying, he's changed. If I stay, he's going to do something to me we will forever regret. Leaving is the only way to save us both."

The mousy girl was gone. Daniela could see a calculating and intelligent young woman behind soulful eyes. Daphne was courageous. Sharing her story had somehow set the timid girl free. She wasn't ashamed of what her father was doing to her. It was more like she felt sorry for him, in a way.

Daniela always thought that by hanging onto her secret, she was protecting herself. But now she saw that it had been strangling her. She rubbed her hand around her neck where she had placed the noose. *This is my second chance.*

"Now, Thomas told me the stuff you were saying and I know you're not well, but we could look out for each other. Like sisters." Daphne smiled.

This took Daniela out of her own head. Daphne was sweet. Her serious eyes told the story of a girl much older than sixteen. They were a misty blue, pensive, and full of wonder. Her features were in direct defiance of the bruise; the black and blue tried unsuccessfully to mar her beauty. Daphne was simply a beautiful girl. She would be easily noticed if they were trying to remain inconspicuous, never mind that she was a white woman who would be seen with a colored man. Daniela searched her memory, remembering that surely it had to be illegal in 1923. Yet further complications.

"I don't know…your father is going to freak the fuck out." Daniela didn't know why she kept stalling. The voice in her head had long since told her she would be taking this girl, no matter the challenge.

Daphne laughed. "Goodness, you'll have to teach me some of your words."

She seemed to be unaffected by the obvious— her father would be furious if he were to catch up with them, and would likely shoot Daniela.

"We will leave tonight. I'll come get you. I have just enough for our train tickets and a little extra to tide us over for a few days." Daphne reached over and hugged Daniela.

"Shit!" Daniela's mind was spinning again. She was going to wind up in jail over a white girl. When had she said yes to Daphne?

Daniela was awakened early, before dawn.

"Shh, I have something for you. These are Thomas's, but will help you blend in better." Daphne handed her a pile of clothes. "Hurry up, but be quiet!"

Daniela did as she was told and dressed in the farm clothes. She carefully placed her things in her backpack and followed Daphne out of the barn. There was a horse tied to a tree, waiting for them. Daphne had thought of everything. They would travel a short distance to Morristown, take a train, and then a ferry into the city.

"Can you ride?"

Daniela shook her head. "No. I had a lesson when I was fifteen, but hated it."

"Alright, you hang onto me." Daphne mounted the horse, reached for Daniela, and hoisted her up like she was hollow.

These farm folks were crazy strong. Daniela hated horses and felt completely out of her element.

"I hate the ferry. Why don't we just take the tunnel or the GWB?" Daniela asked. She was amazed that Daphne could see anything in the total darkness. Starlight was all that she could make out. Even the moon was hiding.

There was no going back now; they were on their own.

"Hush now and hold on. I'll get us out of here." Daphne made a clicking sound to the horse and they took off. "There is a gun in the saddle bag. Can you shoot?"

"I can't even text and walk. I'm afraid shooting a gun while riding horseback is out of the question."

"I have no idea what that means. I don't understand what you're saying sometimes." Daphne laughed softly.

"It means that I'm pretty useless and at the mercy of a sixteen-year-old farm girl from a century back." Daniela laughed too. "Not an easy admission or position to be in. Even if you don't believe I'm from the future right now, I think you'll see for yourself, in time."

"Whether I believe you or not hardly matters. We're in this together."

The horse took an awkward step and Daniela clung to Daphne.

"You see, I told you—you need me and I need you. One wrong step affects us both."

Daniela clung tighter to Daphne. She truly hated horses. She really didn't want an "aha" moment while hanging on for dear life. Daniela thought about a saying her grandmother was fond of, "La carga hace andar al macho." This was certainly a heavy load to bear. But it forced her to move despite feeling completely unprepared for life in 1923. Even the farm clothes she wore would not hide how displaced and awkward she was. She was willing to do anything to get back home.

"I got it." Daniela said, reinforcing her grip around the girl. "Just get us to New York."

"NEW YORK CITY IS EVERYTHING I dreamed it would be. There are cars everywhere and more people than I have ever seen."

"This isn't the Manhattan I'm used to, Daphne. New York is supposed to be the picture of a modern city, but there are still many places that don't allow non-whites," Daniela sulked.

"We have to be careful, Daniela. Try to be more patient."

"I'm confused. I thought all those rules applied to the South."

Finding signs displaying "No Negros, No Mexicans, No Dogs" in Manhattan, of all places, galled her. The reality of being "colored" hit Daniela hard. She hated the looks of disapproval when they went out. By pretending to be a manservant, she found it easier to blend in.

Daphne could only console her.

Daniela cried more and more throughout the nights, until one morning, she remained in bed long after sunrise, unwilling to eat, saying she felt like a failure in life, and in death.

That was two days ago.

Their situation seemed hopeless. They were doomed together or apart, with no solution to this mess. Just getting by on what little they had and without a long-term plan frightened Daniela more every day. She racked her mind but couldn't figure out a way to get back, or understand how she time traveled in the first place. To make things even harder, the responsibility of looking after Daphne created a constant ache in her head leaving her bedridden with angst.

"These are your things." Daphne cupped Daniela's jewelry in her hands. Forcing Daniela to pay attention to her. "You said they were expendable if worse came to worst, but you have to come with me to sell them. I'm not going alone. You can't just stay here in your shell like a turtle. The fresh air will help clear your thoughts."

"No."

"Stop it. Don't be such a ninny. Get dressed, I've had enough. I hate to be stern, but you have a habit of going on and on like a preacher, rambling about damnation, ruin, hippies, racism, civil rights." Daphne's voice trembled with emotion. "I'm trying to be as civil and well mannered as is heavenly possible, but you want better treatment from the whole world. Well, you're not going to get it! Now get dressed, Daniela. I'm at my wit's end." Daphne pulled the wool blanket off Daniela, and pushed her off the bed.

Daniela watched as Daphne walked ahead. Although lost in thought, she kept up with the congestion and fast pace of the financial district. Daniela saw the looks of disapproval whenever she walked too closely to Daphne. She didn't want to find out what would happen if she broke the social norms. Keeping exactly three feet away and walking behind Daphne with her eyes down created the appropriate space.

She remembered learning about a town in Florida called Rosewood. Black people were massacred because a white woman claimed she was raped. Daniela was positive that happened in 1923.... She shivered at the thought. The *New York Times* had pictures of the Ku Klux Klan on display, with parades and social support. Sickening! She felt like a nonentity, out of place most of the time. Here it wasn't just one "Jack" who looked down his nose and treated her like shit at will. The steady stream of hate was more than she was prepared to cope with. It was more unbearable than living lost and alone in 2030.

She noticed other black people around. Most walked a bit slumped over and avoided eye contact with white people. *Be well mannered, be invisible*— the unspoken rule she observed and tried to emulate. Although the situation seemed hopeless, she knew everything would change. Her mere existence was proof—the daughter of a biracial gay couple. Though she often felt it was insignificant, it really mattered. She represented the dream that no one in these times would even dare give voice to. She smiled at the black men working in the stores as she passed.

When they arrived at Maiden Lane, Daniela had the advantage of knowing the shops would one day become the diamond district. Daniela noted the Jewish people seemed slightly friendlier. The women didn't automatically clutch their belongings as she walked by. So strange; now as a man, no one talked to her tits anymore, but no one really looked at her at all. Daniela didn't need to consider which was worse—it all sucked.

"Okay, so I'll just be a little bit. I will try to negotiate the best price."

Daphne stopped in front of the small jewelry shop. Hasidic Jewish men exited as she waited to enter. "Just wait here. And don't take any wooden nickels while I'm gone, ya hear?" Daphne pointed to the sidewalk, playing her role flawlessly.

Daniela crinkled her nose, not knowing what Daphne meant.

"Don't do anything...stupid," Daphne explained under her breath.

"Oh, yes. Of course, ma'am."

Daphne had a bit more practice, existing full-time in 1923. She lived in these harsh times, and seemed to be accepting of how things were. She didn't even mention her father, or any concern about him searching heaven, hell, and earth to find her. Yet another concern of Daniela's as she looked around nervously.

Daniela remembered her dog, Roxie, the Boxer her mothers had given her for Christmas a decade or so back. Every time they walked to the ice cream shop in town, poor Roxie always had a look of betrayal when they left her tethered to the parking meter. Her big brown eyes would plead to come along. Daniela wondered if she looked like Roxie as she paced the sidewalk and stared at her shoes. It was then that she noticed a flyer discarded on the ground:

LOST GIRL
DAPHNE MARIE BUCKLEY
16 years old of Parsippany, New Jersey

Disappearance on November 3. She is 5'4" and 100 pounds with waist-length blonde hair and blue eyes. Last seen with tall Mexican man. Reward offered. Contact Deputy Police Inspector D. Henry, Manhattan police headquarters.

Holy shit—the sketch of Daphne wasn't half bad.

A flying apple, one that narrowly missed her head, interrupted her thoughts.

"Fruit-picking nigger!" the boy-culprit yelled.

He took off running, seemingly fearful of Daniela. If only she could, she would tear his ass UP. Instead, she waited and tried not to panic.

Daniela's thoughts went back to her mothers, the guilt of her suicide attempt, and the grief they must be going through. Did her grandmother know by now? God, it would kill her. Daniela had avoided speaking with her most of the year. She hated lying to her about her life, and her grandmother had a way of cracking her. She berated herself again as she waited for Daphne. It was easier to dwell in the past than to think about her current predicament. It was a way to become invisible, a tactic, she reasoned, to escape both centuries temporarily.

How could she have thought killing herself would have fixed her problems? She ruminated, trying to find the logic. Being without her mothers defined torture. She didn't even want to imagine what could be happening back in 2030. Did they know about the attempted suicide? Did they think she was MIA? Kidnapped? Were police involved? Were her mothers suspects? And this flyer could mean all kinds of consequences. No good came of these musings. The thoughts burned her like a neurotoxin. If she couldn't get back to her mothers and family, would they believe she just didn't care and left them? They would spend the rest of their lives blaming themselves when they had no idea of all she'd been hiding.

Now that she was trapped here, something was shifting. Maybe it was the notion of a second chance. Maybe more. She felt like if she could get through this, she'd understand better who she was, and she'd be stronger back in the real world. God, if she could only get back—instead, of paying this strange penance for her mistakes. Could this be God's plan to teach her gratitude? She felt ashamed now that she had gained an understanding of the big picture.

Message received, God—I'm an asshole.

She thought about the gold necklaces Daphne was selling. One was a gift from her mothers. She gave it to her with such love. Now be the only thing that kept her alive. They needed money desperately, and Daniela couldn't contemplate finding a job and living in this time. She had to get back home. She thought about her beautiful Aunt Sabine. She was from Africa, with skin so dark the other aunts called her the "Negrita de Oro." They said her skin glistened like gold in the Mexican sun and drew everyone to her. She could hardly make it through the market without people coming to touch her — out of reverence, not fear or hatred. Sabine wouldn't survive an hour in Daniela's situation.

There was nothing here for her. She cared for Daphne and wished she could help her more, but she could offer little. Daphne talked about them living as sisters, fantasized about it before they closed their eyes at night. In reality, it would be a cold day in hell before anyone would accept them as sisters, no matter how they tried to rationalize it.

They would each need to fend for themselves eventually. The guilt surfaced in Daniela's chest and spread through her body like a fire. It crippled her with more negative thoughts. Daphne was a good girl, compassionate and caring. The thought of leaving her behind created more devastation. Maybe teleport Daphne to 2030? Yeah, sure, after Daniela worked out a few logistics…. Her hypothesis of being able to transport Daphne and herself from the 1920s through a hole in time to a stranger-than-fiction future was another thing that was taking up needed brain space now. All Daniela could think about was going back to bed and never waking up. That was the easiest option. Daniela paced again, wanting to cry out loud like Roxie used to.

Once outside the jewelry store, Daphne could see that Daniela did not look well. Daphne felt like falling over herself, but Daniela wore a look of despair that encouraged her to get them home as soon as possible.

She's going to leave me…. Daphne tried to dismiss the thought, but the look on Daniela's face stopped her cold—a desolate and heartbroken expression that made Daphne want to risk the danger and embrace her.

"Daniela, you'll be pleased. We can get by for the next month, or even two, if we are extra careful. That's better than either of us had estimated."

Daniela handed her the flyer.

Daphne swallowed the lump in her throat and put on a casual face. She crumpled the flyer and tossed it away from them.

She gave Daniela a tender smile and whispered, "We are going to be okay." She picked up the apple on the ground next to Daniela, rubbed it on the arm of her dress, and walked ahead confidently.

She could hear Daniela grumbling behind her.

SINCE SELLING THE JEWELRY THE day before, Daniela seemed quiet and pensive to Daphne. She watched her lay on the bed, again, unmoving. No more future stories about Daniela's two moms; just an awkward silence filled the room between bouts of crying. Every day, Daphne discovered a little more, though. Her initial shock over the large tattoos that covered Daniela's arm and her curiosity about the earrings in different bodily locations had subsided also. She no longer gawked at Daniela when she changed, even though Daniela did look very thin to Daphne. Daniela explained how things were different in her time, how free women were to express themselves and be however they chose. Daphne didn't understand how that translated to looking like one lived off rabbit stew—poor man's mutton—but who was she to judge. Daniela also explained how underwear would evolve from long johns to the strip of fabric she wore, which looked plain uncomfortable to Daphne.

But, if Daniela's story were true, Daphne felt it would confirm with all certainty that God existed. Perhaps there was another plan for both their lives. It irritated Daphne when Daniela complained about what she had lost with no notion of the gifts she'd gained—like her life. She hadn't died that day. On the other hand, Daphne couldn't conceive of what it must have been like to time travel.

"You need to get up. You need a bath, and we have to get you some new clothes. No one dresses like that around here." Daphne tried to pull Daniela out of bed. Thomas's clothes hung on her like moth-ridden drapes. They were farm clothes, not a sophisticated, tailored suit, as she had seen most men wear in Manhattan. Daphne always felt better after a bath and in her best Sunday dress. Maybe that would do the trick.

"What's the point? I'm already dead." Daniela sighed. "Just leave me. Take what's left of the money and go."

"Stop it! You're not dead! I thought that kind of talk was going to stop." Daphne had the urge to hang Daniela on a clothesline and beat her like a rug. "We promised to look out for one another. I need your help. I won't make it on my own. Now get up!" Daphne pushed her harder. "You need a new suit, and once you're cleaned up, you'll feel better. Get up!"

"Daphne, I can't live as a colored man in 1923. What the hell are we going to do? Just take the money and go back home. I have no plan! Tell your dad I forced you to come with me. Those flyers could be all over Manhattan by now. At least you can go home. I've lost everything," Daniela sobbed. Again. "I just want to die!"

"Do you? Want to die?"

Daniela did not.

"Then hush up! Look what that got you last time. I won't let you try that again. What if you wind up in 1823? Have you considered that….?" Daphne ripped the wool blanket off Daniela, exposing her to the cold. "Now, I accept you cannot do anything and that you don't have a single lonely coin in your pocket, and you're a colored boy in a time when it is not fortuitous to be, but I am not leaving you. I'd rather rot in a jail cell than go back home. I'm never going back." Then Daphne pushed her right off the bed. "If you want to go home, then you have to make it happen. Wallowing is not going to change our situation. If you know everything that is going to happen from that phone of yours, then why don't you use it? You said the texting was the only thing you could do. Whatever that is, why don't you try it." Daphne felt at her wit's end. Again. The daily pep talks felt circular in nature, accomplishing very little. "No one is going to save you, Daniela. You have to fight. You have everything you need to help yourself." Daphne took an exasperated breath. She would drag her along kicking and screaming if she had to.

Something of what she had said seemed to resonate with Daniela. Daphne could see the expression on her face shift. She perked up and reached for her backpack and pulled out the shiny black phone.

Daphne came over and watched her turn it on and press her finger onto small images on the screen. She'd never seen such tiny pictures. Each one had a label underneath like "phone," "messages," "mail," and "camera," but she didn't know how a calendar could fit into the small picture, or what kind of mail would be in a picture. The sharpness of the display made it hard for Daphne to take her eyes off it.

"Well, you're right. I can look up and still access stuff on my phone. How is this working? There are no Internet or cell towers. This is crazy. It actually makes me feel like I'm insane…well, more insane." Daniela managed a small smile. "The signal strength is stronger than it was by the oak tree. There are more bars, but I can't use some apps, or access the Internet, and there are no websites. All my music and pictures are intact."

"You see—I told you." Daphne loved saying that.

Even if she didn't understand all that Daniela said, she did know what it was like to be right all the time. Just holding the phone made Daniela look better, like she was in control of her emotions. Daphne also knew what it was like to long for a mother. She understood that pain. She hurt for Daniela and all that she was going through. She missed her brother, Thomas, in that moment, but he would have understood her decision if he knew all that their father did to her. Daphne wouldn't give up, and if all Daniela needed was a push, she would be there to shove her.

The phone illuminated in Daniela's hand, brighter than any light Daphne had seen, except maybe the full moon in the dead of summer. She projected it off the mirror in the room to give her a better view. It was indescribable to Daphne. Never in her wildest imaginings would she have conceived of how a telephone from her time would one day transform into what Daniela held.

Going through the phone did make Daniela feel normal for a moment. This was the first time in several days that she had held it in her hands. Usually, she had it on her all the time, even when sleeping. She pulled up a map of the city. To her surprise, it was of the location as it was in 1923. It showed her all the streets and parks in the area. She was happy to see some of her favorite stores show up as well. The early versions of the megastores that would someday be were all there. The signal was strong, and she called her home phone. Of course, there was no ringing or answer, but she had to try.

She opened up some pictures and began to show Daphne. Her jaw dropped a little more with every new photo. Daniela took a picture of her with that funny expression on her face, and then displayed it on screen. They both laughed. Using the mirror in the room, she created a slideshow of pictures. It made it feel like they were watching a movie.

"Good Lord, this is amazing!" Daphne continued laughing. She looked at herself in the picture.

"Now do you believe me, Daphne? They don't make these at the market." Daniela took a few more pictures of Daphne and added music to slide show. "It's not the Commodore Orchestra, but it will do."

Daniela smiled as she saw the wonder in Daphne's face. It was like her mind didn't know what to do with the combination of sights and sounds.

"You truly are a time traveler."

"Here, let's take what we call a 'selfie' together." Daniela sat close to Daphne and snapped another picture. "So, usually we post a pic like this on a site for friends and family to see, but…." Daniela looked and saw only the airdrop option on her phone was available. She pressed it for fun and noticed that two people were available to drop to. "This is strange."

"Yes, it's all so strange," Daphne agreed. "Why would you want everyone to see your pictures?" she laughed.

"Who is Lainbites?" Daniela asked aloud. "There is someone near here who has the same technology as me. But how?" Daniela looked over at Daphne, who shrugged.

"Could there be other time travelers around? Do you think they could get me home?" Daniela's voice raised in excitement. "I'm going to send this pic to whoever this is."

Daniela became hopeful. Then, after she sent it, was full of concern. "Oh God, what if they aren't friendly, or try to hurt us?"

"Daniela you're at it again—waiting for someone else to get you home," Daphne reproached. "We could just leave. The city is so large they, or whoever, would never find us."

"If someone could get me home, that would be amazing! I thought you were trying to make me feel better, Daphne. I wouldn't leave you. You could come…." The notion sounded ridiculous as it left her lips, but the most promising situation she had had been in yet in 1923—the existence of a Lainbites, a connection—created an overwhelming dopamine dump in her brain. But she had Daphne to consider, and would haul her along for the ride, if she was game. Someone else with the same technology had to be a time traveler too. She finally felt like she had a chance; they both did.

Daphne held Daniela's hand. "I just don't want you to get your hopes up, or rely on someone else. I—"

Daphne was cut off when the phone vibrated, startling them both.

"Who the fuck are you?" Daniela read the text. Her hands were shaking as she looked at Daphne. "Please pinch me! I need to make sure I'm not dreaming or something. I'm texting in 1923, for God's sake!" Daniela sent a text back with a picture and their names. The moment felt surreal.

"You girls want to party?" Daniela read another text. She took a look at Daphne, whom she could see finally understood what was happening. "It's like a telegraph, a small and portable one. I'm not using Morse code, but pressing letters on the glass, and there are no wires," she explained. "It's amazing to be able to do this here, but how?"

"Swell! Like stories Da used to tell about military radiophones in the war. But I'm sure those had lots of wires. Say yes. Can we see a picture of him, too?"

Daniela showed her the phone. There was a picture of a handsome man on it, winking.

Daphne pinched Daniela hard. "You're not dreaming!"

DETECTIVE HICKS HAD A BAD feeling from the moment he pulled up to the large home on Wolf Drive. He was assigned to the case because of the high-profile nature of the family. Apparently, the mothers of this kid were well-liked and politically connected. One of them had called the chief and requested the very best, and Detective Hicks had a way of breaking cases like no one else. Since retiring from the police force three years ago, his private investigative services were in high demand. Pulling himself from his other cases meant this family had some serious influence and money. Hicks had plenty of experience with missing person cases like this from his long career, and he knew what to expect when he knocked on the door.

The woman who answered the door looked exhausted. Her puffy, swollen eyes were surrounded by red blotches and broken blood vessels evidencing her devastation. She held a wad of used tissues in her hand and was wiping her drippy nose. She didn't look like the pretty, put-together lady that was in the papers all the time for her various philanthropic events and endeavors. In those pictures, she always looked like a model—perfectly posed, with a flawless smile on her beautiful face. As soon as the detective flashed his badge, she lost control again.

"Mrs. Delgado, I'm Detective Hicks. I'm sorry to have to speak with you under these circumstances. I need to collect some information from you and your wife. May I come in?"

Monica could only nod. She barely had the strength to speak, let alone rehash the details of her daughter's disappearance. "I just want Daniela home. Who would take her? This is a nightmare that just keeps getting worse." Monica took a short breath. "She didn't try to kill herself—Daniela would never do that."

She turned around, leaving the Detective to come in behind her.

"Understand, we're not ruling anything out at this time." Hicks took out his notepad and took a moment to survey the house. There were pictures of Daniela everywhere, lining the walls, the stairway, and even the small table in the foyer. She looked to be the only child this couple had, and she was clearly adored. The family was devastated and Hicks knew cases like this never ended well. He had strong instincts about people and could quickly gauge a situation.

They walked into a large kitchen, where the other Mrs. Delgado was pacing while on the phone. He couldn't hear who she was speaking with, but had a feeling it was the police chief.

"Yes, he just arrived. Yes, thank you for sending me your best man. I appreciate it, George." She looked over at Hicks as she spoke.

Hicks knew the chief wasn't on a first name basis with anyone. He had underestimated how important this family was to the police department and community. He felt his stomach turn from the pressure of this case. Emma gave him an uneasy feeling, like meeting a girlfriend's father for the first time. She was a legend all over the state, a decorated army veteran who was active with the city council and always nominated to any board that had an open seat. Everyone respected her opinions and her honesty. Rumors were that she would be running for office next year, with many prominent donors ready to make her next home the governor's mansion.

"Daniela was home a bit early from school for Thanksgiving break, yes?" he asked Monica.

"Yes, Daniela didn't have to take a few of her midterms. Her GPA is excellent." Monica struggled to answer. "She's in her junior year at Georgetown. She has a boyfriend and lots of friends. Her life is pretty perfect. She would never try to hurt herself or run away." Monica stopped short, her voice cracking.

"Monica's right," Emma said, ending her phone call. She gave Hicks a firm handshake. "I know what they found at the park, but she would never try to kill herself. She told me she was going for a run. She's made that run a thousand times before."

Emma looked at the detective. She seemed to be hoping he would not try to convince her otherwise. Hicks sensed that she was visibly hiding her panic.

"Besides, if she had tried to hang herself, we would have found her," Emma continued. "I know the rope was strung up on the tree,

66

but Daniela is gone. Somebody must have abducted her. Maybe the person who took her left suddenly and changed his plan."

The detective nodded. "What makes you think a man took her? Did she have any male enemies? Is there someone who may have had a grudge with her?"

"Daniela is tall and pretty strong," Emma said. "If a woman had tried to take her, she would have easily been able to defend herself. It had to be a man who overpowered her or something."

"There were no signs of a struggle anywhere in a three-mile radius. Everything we have tells us she ran there and stopped at that tree. The police are running the rope for prints and examining the whole area. If your suspicion is right, we'll find the person who took her." Hicks hid the doubt in his voice. He knew deep down this kid had wanted to kill herself. "Can I have her electronics? Anything she may have used last night? Also, I'll need recent photos, and all of her contacts from school. Did you know her boyfriend?"

Monica walked out of the kitchen.

"Things weren't great with the boyfriend. His name is Jack. His father is a senator in Alabama. Conner is the last name. Old money and close-minded is how Daniela described the family." Emma pointed to Daniela's MacBook. "I want to be informed right away if you find something, Detective. We're working with you because you understand the need for discretion."

"Yes, of course. I'll take good care of these. Do you mind if I take a look at her room? Was there anything missing? Did she pack anything unusual? The report said she had a backpack."

Monica returned with the pictures. Emma held her hand.

Hicks looked at both of them as he thumbed through the pictures they gave him. "Her hair is long in all of these pictures; the report described her as having short hair, about 5'9", and hazel eyes."

"Yes, it was a bit of a shock when she got home last night. She had cut it the day before—said she wanted a change. She looked cute. We just don't have any pictures with her new haircut."

"No problem, we can alter these," he replied. "My report also mentions her tattoos and the jewelry she was wearing. Do you have any pictures?"

"They're all in there. She has an arm sleeve tattoo. It started above her wrist. As far as packing anything unusual, we can't say. There's nothing missing from her room except for the clothes she was wearing. And three gold necklaces—she always wears those. And of course her phone...and earbuds, a charger, and maybe a change of clothes were gone—she always keeps an extra set of workout clothes in her bag. Nothing out of the ordinary."

Monica nodded. "Her purse and wallet are here. If she were running away, she would need money, don't you think?"

"Okay, I'll be just a few minutes in her room. Could you show me up?" Hicks ignored the last question. He didn't want to further distress this family.

Monica stepped forward to lead the detective up the stairs.

It looked like a suite in a fancy hotel. The kid had it all. Yet, as he looked around, Hicks felt that Daniela was profoundly unhappy.

The feelings began to choke him. The room had a sterile feel to it. Traditionally, a college kid's room back home has more...life. Photos of friends, awards, posters, books, stuffed animals—a mishmash of items that reveal information about the journey from adolescence to adulthood. This room looked like it was staged for an open house. Come to think of it, the whole house was perfect.

Type As, maybe. He still felt strongly that Monica was clueless. She didn't have anything to do with Daniela's disappearance. Emma gave him the impression she had something to hide, but he decided she wasn't a criminal.

He took some pictures and left.

EMMA'S HANDS TREMBLED ONCE THE detective left. Her mind was racing, and she felt a panic attack coming on. Her pulse grew irregular and she struggled to breathe. She looked at her wife and whispered, "I have to, Monica."

Monica knew that look. "No! Listen to me—we have to let the police do their job. I do not want to involve your mother. Every time you even think of her, you get like this." Monica shook her head in disbelief. The *last* thing they needed was her mother-in-law. "You can't run to your mother, not after all the progress we've made. We can deal with this. Just give the police time to do their job. Please, baby."

"Only twenty-four hours, Monica. Then, I have to make the call." Emma's voice shook as the panic attack took hold.

Monica filled a glass with tap water and rushed to Emma's side. "Please. You've been doing so well these last four years. Think about what your therapist said—you need strong boundaries with your mother. Let's give it forty-eight hours." Monica hugged Emma and wiped the tears streaming down her face. "Shh, we're going to find her."

Inside, Monica was terrified.

Two days later, there was still no lead or explanation for the disappearance. A news conference had been held and volunteers were combing the park. The private investigator remained hard at work, but nothing turned up.

Emma could feel her hope of finding Daniela alive draining with each passing hour. She was crumbling. She had to make the call, despite the intense fear that coursed through her body.

Emma walked into her study. If she made the call from here, at least she would be surrounded by all her achievements on the walls. Monica had hung up Emma's medals from her service in the military, plaques from the town, her degrees, and anything and everything that she had earned. At least in this room, she would be reminded that she wasn't the disappointment her mother always claimed. After failing to dial the phone for five minutes, she called for Monica to come in for moral support.

With her soul mate by her side, Emma took a deep breath and dialed.

"Bueno. ¿Quién es?" her mother demanded.

Emma swallowed hard. Her throat was suddenly dry. "Mama, it's me." She bit her lip, waiting for her mother to recognize her voice.

"Ah ha, after four years you remembered that you have a mother, huh?" Anaya's voice was cutting.

The simple phrase was a dagger. The only way Emma had been able to maintain boundaries with her mother was to cut her out completely.

"What do you want?" Anaya continued.

Emma felt like someone sucked all the oxygen out of the room. She struggled to speak. "Mama...I have some bad news. It's Daniela.... Daniela is missing, and we need help finding her." Emma's voice trembled. She looked up at the wall in front of her. She'd earned two purple hearts and a medal for her bravery in combat. What a crock of shit. Her mother, who was 5'3", had Emma's knees knocking in fear. "Mama, please, will you help us?" She felt like she was five again.

"I knew you would call today. There was a black raven in the garden that was squawking all morning. It made no sense and irritated me. As soon as I got near it, it flew away, only to return and continue to whine. Mmm...."

Anaya always made that noise when she spoke. The "mmm" was like a confirmation of something, a question she had asked and answered for herself. It was Anaya's way of saying "I told you so" to whomever she was demeaning.

"Of all my children, you are the worst. I had such high hopes for you, Emma."

Emma couldn't understand. What was it that hurt her mother so much? Was it that she was a lesbian? Or that she was happy?

These are the questions she pondered for years in therapy. She left home for an amazing opportunity. Her mother never understood. She wanted Emma to stay in Mexico, and never forgave her for leaving. Fuck, she was so tired of the nonsense.

Enough already. For a moment, she felt a brief glimmer of bravery and considered biting back.

Then her mother spoke again. "Come alone. I don't want that woman you're with here. Mmm…."

Emma reached out and grabbed Monica's hand. "Mom, she's my wife. I can't—"

"She doesn't understand our ways! She never will. I told you already. May God bless you and keep you safe." Anaya hung up the phone, unconcerned with the blaze she had left to burn in Emma's home.

Monica was looking at Emma with hopeful eyes. "Well? What did she say?"

Emma started sobbing. "I don't fucking know!" She tried to regain her composure. "She hates me. It's the same shit over and over again."

Monica hugged her tightly. "Please, just tell me what she said."

"I'm a disappointment. I broke her heart, and the fact that I left is killing her. Nothing I say will ever make sense to her, and she will never accept us. She's going to help me, but she doesn't want you to come. She doesn't care what I've done with my life, or all that we've worked for. I mean, Jesus, Monica! What didn't she say?"

Emma didn't realize she was yelling. She wanted to smash something, anything.

"Emma, you were on the phone with her for two minutes. I timed it. How did she manage to say all of that?" Monica was confused. She hadn't heard any yelling or arguing. It had been a calm conversation, from what she could tell.

"You will never understand!" Emma shouted her mother's words at Monica. She was disappointed that her mother's venom had reached them. The anger was loose in the room, smothering them both now.

"My God, Emma, you sound just like her." Monica backed away. A look of frustration and pain settled on her face. "I'm calling Dr. Casey. You need to talk to him before you decide to go see her." Monica left the room.

Emma was disgusted with herself—Monica was right. There was nothing she could do. Emma was sure her mother could help in some way to find Daniela.

DETECTIVE HICKS STARED AT HIS email, dumbfounded. He knew it was his ass on the line. Everyone told him Emma Delgado wasn't a person of interest. The police chief, the local detective handling the case, and even the governor vouched for her. Hicks had a sinking feeling in his stomach. Why would Emma want to travel to Mexico at a time like this? What about Monica—why wasn't she going too? Something didn't feel right. It made no sense, but Hicks felt that once he gave the approval for Emma to travel to Mexico, she wouldn't return. The pressure from everyone was making him bend. He called the Delgado residence one last time.

"Hello, Monica. It's Detective Hicks."

"Emma's not here. I can have her call you when she gets home."

"No, it's okay, Monica. I actually want to talk with you. I'm concerned about this trip Emma is taking. I have to say, the timing is unfortunate. We could turn up a new lead at any time, and we may really need her here."

"I understand. I'm not happy about this, either. I'll be here for anything you may need. She feels strongly that telling her mother personally will be easier. She's elderly. Emma worries she won't take the news well."

Monica spoke like she had rehearsed this speech many times. She must have used it with other friends who were asking why Emma was leaving. Monica may have believed it herself now, making the lie easier to sell. Hicks was still unconvinced.

Monica stared at the phone. Even on speaker, the detective sounded so stern. She was sure he could tell she was babbling. Monica had never lied to the police before. She really didn't have a clue why Emma was so convinced that Anaya could do something to find Daniela faster than the police. She was tired of arguing about it. All her pleading and tears were in vain. Emma had made her decision, and there was no swaying her.

Monica's only solace was that Emma promised to return in a few days. She swallowed her disappointment and focused on the detective. She would have days alone to cry. But she had to keep it together a few moments longer. This was important to Emma.

"Uh huh…." Hicks must be a master at detecting lies. "I have some concerns about the address she gave me. It doesn't seem to be showing up on any map. I need to know exactly where she'll be staying. Everyone is considered a person of interest."

"I have the same address. I can confirm it with her later. That's the address we send mail to, and I've been there myself. I can promise you, it's an actual house."

Monica laughed a little. It was a rural area, but the house was easy to locate. What kind of lunatic had a ten-foot wall of cement and rock surrounding their home, with an iron gate at the entrance? Her always-accepting and welcoming mother-in-law, that's who.

Monica could hear Hicks take a deep breath. "Okay, I'll approve it. Let her know, if she's not back in a week, I will personally go there for her. That's a promise."

Monica laughed again, trying to seem casual. "Of course. Trust me, if she's not back in a week, I'll go with you. I appreciate your concern. Emma will return as soon as possible. She doesn't want to spend a minute longer than she has to there. She hates Mexico."

"Alright, I have your word then. One week, and then we'll be knocking on her mother's door. I'm fighting the urge to book the airfare right now, but I'll take your word for it." He hung up the phone.

Monica cried in relief.

ANAYA WATCHED HER DAUGHTER UNLOAD her bags from the cab parked outside the large iron gates that surrounded the hacienda. Emma looked as if she had been carrying the world on her shoulders.

Stupid girl. She is only tormenting herself.

Had Emma listened to her mother, all of this could have been avoided. Emma ran from everything that had to do with Anaya. And Anaya didn't have time for people who couldn't keep promises, or accept their destiny. If this wasn't about Daniela.... It didn't matter now. Emma was here, and she would never leave again. It was time for her to join the coven and lead it.

Anaya walked over to the gate. She was determined to make this as difficult as possible. Her daughter would not understand the severity of her actions any other way. Emma was the type that had to be hit in the face with something before she would believe it was real. Anaya opened the door and stared for a moment.

"Buenos dias, Mama." Emma spoke in a defeated voice and then looked at her mother in disbelief. "You look better than ever. You have not aged a day since I last saw you."

Anaya extended her hand. Emma grabbed it gently and kissed it several times.

Anaya took a deep breath to steady herself. Emma's brazen bravery and headstrong nature was so much like her own. For this reason, she knew exactly how to shake her like no one else.

"Emma, you look terrible." Anaya touched Emma's cheek. She wiped away the tears that streamed down her daughter's face and looked into her hazel eyes. In that gaze, Anaya could hear all the words Emma could not express. It was a silent understanding between a mother and daughter. Anaya knew Emma was sorry for not speaking to her for so long and that her heart was heavy with pain and worry for Daniela.

Anaya pulled Emma close and embraced her. "Jah, mi niña. Todo va estar bien."

Emma sobbed in her arms. Anaya held her like when she was a little girl, and assured her everything would be all right.

"We have much work to do. Leave your bags here; you will be leaving soon." Anaya released Emma and directed her toward the kitchen.

Emma quickly wiped her tears away and did as Anaya asked. Now that she was home, there were unspoken rules Emma knew well: obey, respect, and understand that her mother's command was law. If Anaya said the sky was black, then it was. No questions, no problems. Being a veteran, Emma knew how to take orders, and this would be like another tour of duty. If she wanted to return home unscathed, then she had to follow Anaya's rules.

She followed behind carefully. The home where her mother, aunts, and two uncles lived had not changed since her last visit with Daniela seven years ago. Being here was like taking a step back in time. It was a large Spanish Colonial-style home that had been in her family for hundreds of years. Growing up in the massive home had been difficult, and often lonely.

The outer courtyard was Emma's favorite part. With its lush garden, it reminded her of a secret oasis. The inside of the house had twenty-foot beamed ceilings and hand-painted floors with Mayan hieroglyphs she did not understand. The carved wooden doors and beautiful arched windows allowed sunlight to illuminate the home. It reminded her of a church with its silent beauty.

She could smell the food in the kitchen. She imagined her aunts had stayed up all night making it all fresh for her. When she walked in, everyone was sitting around the old oak kitchen table, smiling. Her aunt Valencia adjusted her glasses. Lola, Sabine, and her uncles were already setting out the plates. "Volver, Volver" by Vicente Fernandez played in the background. The song confirmed her mother's victory.

"Mija! Mija!" Aunt Lola ran over and hugged Emma tightly. "Where is Monica? Why didn't she come with you?"

The look on Emma's face confirmed that Anaya had a hand in Monica being absent. Anaya couldn't stand Monica, blaming her for taking Emma away.

Aunt Lola had always Emma's favorite. Lola gave Anaya a glare for not letting Monica come.

"She had to stay and deal with the police. I'm sorry, Tia, next time. This is a short trip."

Lola seemed visibly surprised.

Emma wasn't sure what shocked Lola more—the mention of the police or the brevity of her visit. Emma knew her phone call was a hot topic in the house and that Anaya told everyone Daniela was missing. Her other aunts and her two uncles came to hug Emma and exchange well-wishes. Her uncles were identical twins; Emma could never tell them apart, but they didn't seem to mind. They had been born mute and expressed themselves through paintings that were displayed around the house.

Emma's stomach emitted an audible growl, which reminded her that she had not eaten. Although she had no desire for food, her body was running on autopilot. The mole and tortillas smelled amazing, triggering her natural response to gorge. There was fresh cheese on the table, with crema to drizzle on whatever needed that extra punch.

Anaya allowed Emma to get three good bites in before she interrupted. "Tonight, you will go to Cuernavaca. Do you remember the cemetery near the xocalo?"

Emma's stomach sank. Suddenly, the chocolaty spice and cream was not sitting well. She didn't have time for this bullshit. "No. I just want to know if Daniela is alive and what's the best way to find her."

Emma looked around the table. All eyes were down, avoiding contact. Her aunts and uncles were prepared for the showdown. They looked uncomfortable in their seats and watched with anticipation.

"After you do this, we will know for sure. It's the only way. It has to be you," Anaya persisted. "If you're scared, Sabine can go with you." Anaya looked over at Sabine, who nodded.

Sabine was technically not Emma's blood aunt; she was more of a big sister. Sabine had lived with them for as long as Emma could remember. They'd had a weird competition since childhood because Sabine was Anaya's favorite. Emma always felt that in the eyes of her mother, Sabine could do no wrong. Anaya's insinuation that Emma was scared was yet another underhanded insult.

"Mi negrita de oro, go with her, please," Anaya asked in her sweetest voice.

Emma burned with jealousy. Her mother never spoke to her with such tenderness or called her precious black gold. She hated feeling like this. "No, I can go alone. It's fine. Just tell me what you need." Emma smiled at Sabine as she spoke to her mother.

They both understood the smile was meant as an insult. They had been playing this game with Anaya for a long time. It was easy for Emma's mother to play along, like making tamales from scratch, which Anaya could do in her sleep. Just mentioning Sabine doing something for her always twisted Emma's sensibilities from rational to an obsessive need to please.

"You will go to the cemetery and find the grave of a woman who has been buried for at least ten years. She needs to have been a mother. I need you to bring me her bones or ashes, along with the cross she was buried with and dirt from her grave."

"Are you fucking crazy? You want me to do what?" Emma had been asked in the past to do strange things for her mother, but this was by far the worst. The look on Anaya's face made Emma's stomach continue to sink. She fought the urge to vomit.

"I don't believe in this stuff. I don't see how any of this will help me find Daniela. My daughter is missing, damn it! Don't you get it? I don't have time for this bullshit. It's complete nonsense to desecrate a grave for a sick game." Emma took a breath. That had taken all of her courage. Speaking to her mother like that in front of the family was a huge risk.

"I'm not asking you to believe. It's better if you don't. Like I said, Sabine can go with you, but she can't do it for you. Without this, I'm afraid I can't help you."

Emma knew she had to make the choice. The voice inside her head screamed not to. Emma's horror at what she was being asked to do made her want to cry in despair.

Anaya waited patiently for Emma to decide. The silence and tension in the room was stifling.

Dear God, Emma thought to herself, *can I really do this? Will it even matter?*

Doubt filled her. Monica would never have understood this. Emma barely did herself. She knew it was hard for Monica to believe her mother could be of any help, especially since Anaya never left the house. Emma was sure it was agoraphobia, but her mother never sought help. She wondered how, after so many years, Anaya could just sit at home while the world around her changed. She had missed so much with her illness.

Her whole life, Emma witnessed people from all over Mexico coming and seeking her mother's counsel on everything—illness, pregnancy, sorcery, cures. Anaya was a curandera, a person who heals through the use of folk remedies. There were things she did that had no explanation. Anaya had the ability to help people, and was apparently really good at it. She was the last resort when all other options failed, an efficacious miracle worker who was prompt and powerful. People would come to see her on their knees, like they would the Virgin of Guadalupe. The townspeople called Anaya la Niña Bonita, but Emma overheard whispers of the name Santa Muerte. Exaggerations and gossip, she was sure. Anaya didn't care for either name, preferring to be simply known as a Cabrona—a true battle-axe, not to be trifled with.

The entire town always treated Emma with a sense of reverence for being Anaya's daughter. Emma worked hard to be that type of person in her own town and state. She was close, but never like her mother. Maybe it was a fantasy that, one day, Anaya would need her and seek her out. Emma hated the continual cycle of trying and fail-ing to gain her mother's approval. Now desperate, Emma would try anything to get Daniela back.

"Okay. I will go tonight and come back as soon as I can. Can you tell me if she's still alive, at least?"

Anaya reached out and held hands, encouraging everyone to do the same. Emma reluctantly clasped Sabine's hand. She smirked, ap-parently enjoying this as much as her mother. They quietly formed a circle. Anaya chanted as everyone bowed their heads:

"I am woman of the earth
United we are strong
One of us lingers, lost
Holy Mother
A brilliant star
That serves you
Give us the answer we need."

Anaya closed her eyes for a long moment. "Yes, she's alive."

Emma released the breath she had been holding since Daniela's disappearance. She felt her shoulders lower. Her daughter was alive. She let the words resonate within her and cried. Daniela was alive, and maybe she could really find her. It was the boost of energy she needed.

"Fine. I need to borrow a car. I'll leave now and find a grave. The sooner we get this over with, the better. I can't be here long."

Emma grabbed the keys from Sabine. The drive to Cuernavaca was a long one.

13

AFTER SOME RESEARCH AT THE library, Emma identified the grave of Beatriz Ramirez. Much like Anaya, Cuernavaca was stuck in time. Modern technology was limited; Internet reception touch and go, at best. Burial records and plots had to be searched out the old-fashioned way, one large, dusty book at a time.

Emma discovered Beatriz Ramirez was a mother of ten. She had died in 1973, and was buried in an aboveground tomb with a tree next to it that provided excellent cover. An ideal situation for grave robbing, if ever there was an ideal. The name on the crypt had been worn away after so many years in the unkempt cemetery, but the research helped. The grave was undisturbed. Her research also indicated that once all the plots were taken, people were buried on top of each other, or bodies were removed to make room for paying families. Cemetery plots had to be paid for yearly in Cuernavaca, or a family risked losing a loved one forever. Beatriz's family had lovingly maintained her burial spot for fifty-seven years—not an easy task for some families.

Exactly how illegal is this? Emma's mood crumbled. Her con-
science weighed heavily. It seemed it was always about levels of
strange, grotesque, and just plain wrong with her mom.

A locked iron gate surrounded the tomb and a white marble slab
covered it. The slab looked like it weighed several hundred pounds.
Still, sliding it off would be manageable, Emma reasoned. It was by
far easier to access an aboveground tomb than to spend the evening
digging. A nearby eucalyptus tree provided an excellent location for
Emma to hide her supplies—a wooden cross she hammered together herself, a messenger bag, and two quart-sized mason jars.

Luckily, this was Mexico. For a few hundred dollars, she could
pay one of the attendants in the morning to assist her with opening
the grave. There was no need for an exhumation license or a legal
petition, which would have been needed in the states. Likely no
questions would even be asked. Most Mexican people, with the exception of her mother, had strong superstitions about desecrating
graves. With any luck, the attendant would open the grave and leave
her alone to do her despicable work. There were only a few hours
before the Panteon de La Leona opened. Emma slept in her car and
waited.

Early in the morning, Emma held a warm cup of coffee as she
waited for the gates to open. The aroma of cinnamon in her drink
helped to ready her senses for the task ahead. She wrapped up the
small talk with the street vendor over coffee and churros, and approached the entrance. There were vendors setting up flowers and

candles to sell to mourners. A man was busy sweeping the entrance and ordering children to have buckets ready for the people who came. A mourner this early was an unusual occurrence. The coffee vendor warned Emma not to go into the cemetery until after 10:00 a.m.

"Espantan," she had said. Emma didn't doubt it. The graveyard dated back to 1885. She was sure there were ghosts lurking.

Francisco, the young attendant, was happy to help Emma. He was the one in charge. She explained she was a relative, and wanted to leave ashes in the grave of a baby who died recently. Emma had an elaborate story ready, but found it unnecessary. He went into the small office and looked up Beatriz Ramirez. The hundred-dollar bill was sufficient. Money trumps superstition, in Mexican—or any—culture. He grabbed the key that unlocked the gate surrounding the crypt. Francisco walked with her to the grave, sharing ghost stories along the way. He was used to handling slabs of marble efficiently. Before she knew it, Emma was standing alone at the open grave of Beatriz.

"Let it air out for a little while," Francisco suggested as he placed the money in his shirt pocket. "The smell is strong." He picked up the crowbar and smiled at Emma before leaving.

"Strong" was not the word Emma would have used to describe the consuming scent the crypt released. It was an ancient smell of rot and musk, like a dead deer on the side of the road on a hot summer day. Emma gagged by the tree, convulsed, and held onto the low branches for support. She swallowed her thick saliva repeatedly, trying to quell the urge to vomit. Her hands trembled from the thought of what she needed to do next.

Emma placed her arm over her nose, but still felt the pungent scent of death permeate and overwhelm all her senses as she approached. She steeled herself; Emma would do this and worse if it meant having Daniela back unharmed.

She looked inside, unprepared for all the silver hair that was in the grave around the body. It was the kind of hair a child would reach out and touch without asking permission. It was so shiny it glistened, and had to be five feet long or more. A gold cross lay across her chest, on her a thin and fraying blue dress.

With a heavy heart, Emma snatched the cross and placed it in her messenger bag. She continued to gag as she opened one of the jars. She would need to reach back inside several times to get dust and bits of bones.

The face on the corpse was well preserved. The vacant eyes judged her. Emma could make out all of the features on the taut and browned skin. Beatriz's white teeth were still intact. The rest of the body was in various stages of decay, and with a small squeeze the leg bones turned to dust. Emma filled one glass jar with the decay, and another with dirt from around the tomb. She replaced the gold cross with a wooden one she had hidden the night before by the tree.

Please forgive me…. Forgive my sins…. Count not my transgressions but, rather, my tears of repentance…. Finding my child alive is all I want. I am so sorry. Surely, you will understand…?

Talking to the corpse put her over the edge. Emma ran to the tree to empty her stomach. Until she observed herself wiping her hands repeatedly on the grass, she had not believed the moment was real. Why the fuck didn't she bring some gloves? Next time she would pack some and a mask. *"Next time?" You asshole…. What, are you going to dig up a grave for Christmas or something?*

On the surface, she felt a small sense of relief it was over. But nothing could cleanse her soul of this crime. Her prayer of forgiveness for this ethical infraction was insufficient.

Emma had a long drive ahead of her. It allowed plenty of time to berate herself and curse her mother, which she did in that order.

It was just after 2:00 a.m. when she arrived at her mother's house. The entire ride back, she had tried to imagine what her mother would do with the ashes. Most of what Emma had overheard as a child seemed outlandish when she tried to reason through it. She had always been afraid to ask her mother about the memories. Years of experience taught her that ignorance was bliss when it came to her mother's work.

Anaya was waiting for Emma by the front door. "That was fast, mija. I wasn't sure you would have it in you." Anaya smiled.

Emma was shocked. Grave robbing was the secret to getting into her mother's good graces? Well, the look on her face was a welcome change from the usual disappointment.

"Are you cold, Mama? The hair on your arms is standing on end. Here, take this jacket." Emma could see a shiver run through her mom, but Anaya declined the jean jacket. Emma's curiosity about what would happen next superseded her anger toward her mother, for the moment.

"Don't you feel it? The cold draft of death you bring with you, Emma? You cannot come inside. We fixed you a bed in the casita." Anaya pointed to the small guesthouse and walked with Emma toward it.

Emma's heart sank. The casita was full of old memories.

"Before you go to bed, place the cross directly under your bed. It should face the same direction that you sleep. Scatter the ashes next to you on the bed in the shape of a cross." Anaya looked at Emma to make sure she understood.

Emma knew better than to question her; she simply repeated the instructions, so her mother felt comfortable with leaving her to the task.

"Say three Hail Marys before you go to sleep. That is most important. Call for me if you need me. We will do our part inside." Anaya kissed Emma and left her by the door of the casita.

She had already said a dozen prayers, but surely three more couldn't hurt.

"HAIL MARY, FULL OF GRACE. The Lord is with thee. Blessed art thou amongst women, and blessed is the fruit of thy womb...." Emma mumbled on, but fell into a profound sleep before making it to prayer's end. She was deep into a Daniela dream, which was not uncommon, when she felt someone enter her space. She focused on this intrusion and swung her subconscious away from the dream, sensing this presence staring right at her. They were nose to nose. A cold, prickling sensation trickled through her body. She jumped in her sleep and woke herself up.

Startled, she looked around the room and saw nothing but darkness. A small window emitted a diagonal beam of dusty light across the bedroom. The full-size bed was in the center of the room, allowing her an unobstructed view of the entire space.

Emma saw nothing. She looked at the door; it was still closed. No one had entered.

She turned carefully to her side, so as not to disturb the ashes. Emma was determined to go back to sleep despite the feeling of being watched. She snuggled her face in the pillow and closed her eyes. The dream had unnerved her, and she remained alert. She opened an eye to scan the room and slowly talked herself out of her hyper-vigilant state with a meditation Dr. Casey had given her in therapy. She focused on her breathing and started to fall back asleep. In the stillness, she could still hear breathing that wasn't her own. Emma remained silent, listening. She felt the opposite side of the bed sink in, as if someone had just sat next to her.

Perhaps her mother had come to check on her, she reasoned. She sucked in her fear and rolled over. Again, there was nothing—just a feeling that someone was…there.

When she turned back around, a strange face was suddenly blowing icy breath in hers. Emma's body trembled with cold and fear. She could not make out any features. She screamed as she backed away.

"Who are you?!" the face roared.

Emma couldn't answer. She scurried back farther when she felt a force, like horizontal gravity, try and yank her legs forward. But then, with a loud thud, she was pulled right off the bed. Disoriented, Emma tried to stand up, but was shoved back to the floor.

"Give me my cross!"

Emma placed her hands over her ears. The voice screamed again, but Emma couldn't understand it. It was too shrill.

"Mama! Mama!" Emma called as the shadow in the room ran toward her. "Mama, help me!"

The face was, again, inches from hers. It kept yelling for the cross, over and over. Emma was in a corner with her trembling hands muffling her ears. The room had become incredibly cold. She could see her breath as she panted. She couldn't take much more of the screaming from whoever it was who knew about the cross she dug up. Emma was unable to determine if she was still somehow dreaming. ...But this couldn't be real.

All Emma could see was a black shadow and objects intermittently flying around the room, like plates or pictures or shoes.... It didn't make sense.

The urge to piss herself was strong, yet she managed to control it. She felt frozen, like a photograph. The door swung open and shut, as if someone considered coming in but saw the commotion, thought better of it, and left. Emma wanted to scream for help again, but couldn't. Between protecting her head from getting clobbered and not pissing herself, all her energy was consumed.

"Basta!" Anaya yelled over the spirit. Anaya crouched down and helped Emma up. "You need to control it. You must tell it what you want!"

"What the hell is going on?" Emma knees buckled. She felt like she was trapped inside the funnel of a tornado and her mother was a safe anchor. Anaya hoisted her back up again.

"How the hell am I supposed to do that? What is it?"

Emma's heart was a deafening pound in her ears and her hands kept shaking. She had a hunch that whatever was in the room was not of this world. But now that Mom had come to the rescue, her hunch evolved into more of a primal knowing.

"Who did you dig up? She's here and she's pissed!" Anaya answered. "I can't help you. This is your ghost. Close your eyes so you can see her." Anaya gave Emma a quick shake to get her attention. "Do it!"

Emma closed her eyes. She jumped back when she saw the face again and looked at her mother in disbelief. She closed her eyes once more and told herself to be brave and study this ghost thing. She saw a small woman, about five feet tall, wearing that flimsy blue dress. She was also wearing a white rebozo, a traditional shawl, around her shoulders.

"Beatriz!" Emma shouted.

The small woman stomped her feet and raised a fist. Then Beatriz ran toward Emma and punched her in the mouth.

Emma stumbled with the hit. "I need your help. Once you help me, I will return your cross and ashes. I promise."

"Tell her if she doesn't help you, you'll burn them!" Anaya suggested in a hateful tone. Her mother was not at all afraid.

"What would that do to her?" Emma asked, holding her lip. It was swelling, and felt sticky and warm. Beatriz had split it—she packed quite a punch for a woman who'd been dead for over fifty years. Emma had crushed Beatriz's femur between her thumb and index finger early that morning, and now her lip was split and bleeding from the right hook of this "figment of her imagination."

"She needs them beside her in the tomb, in order to continue to possess the ability to visit her children and watch over them. She needs all three; if we break the link, she won't be able to do that anymore."

"I don't want to hurt anyone. I just want her help," Emma sighed. "I don't want to keep her from her children. It's hell. It's hell to miss a child, to not know how they are... where they are...if they are...." Emma collapsed into a heap, tears streaming down her face, mixing with the blood from her lip.

"Then convince her. Tell her we need her to find Daniela. Tell your story—mother to mother, Emma. She will understand that language." Anaya ducked as a lamp flew past them.

Emma didn't know who was scarier—the ghost or her mom.

Dear God.

Her instincts told her this was something her mother had done before. She was so calm, walking her through this like she did her signature chicken soup recipe when Emma left for college.

Anaya was stern, hoping it would force Emma to speak to Beatriz. "Hurry! She is strong for a spirit. She may almost be an angel, and we don't want to mess with an angel." Anaya watched as Beatriz continued to throw things around the room, smashing everything in sight.

Right, Emma thought. She didn't understand why an angel would be a bad thing. Perhaps an angel could help them. This whirl of things around the room mirrored her mind, thoughts reeling around like objects with no explanation, no safe place to land. Most of the time spent with Mom was like one giant leap of faith, and this was no exception.

Emma closed her eyes and spoke out loud to Beatriz. "Please…I need your help. My daughter is missing and I need to find her…."

The more she spoke, the calmer Beatriz became.

"Good. Relate to her as a mother. She was a good person in life, I can feel it." Anaya held Emma's hand.

As Emma's heartfelt plea progressed, the room grew still. The soft sound of Emma sobbing was all that remained. A strong smell of flowers filled the little house.

"Good, Emma; she's going to help you." Anaya smiled with jubilance. "You surprised me, mi niña. You are stronger than I imagined."

Anaya closed her eyes and saw Beatriz clearly. She could sense Beatriz was of very strong character, and in life had been a tough woman. Anaya could respect that and knew they were equals in many ways. All of them, as mothers, would risk anything to be with their children, and women with nothing to lose were dangerous indeed.

Beatriz was even tinier than Anaya. Her long silvery hair was black and in a tight bun, a futile attempt to tame curls that escaped around her forehead. She had dark eyes, the color of midnight, with long lashes accentuating their almond shape. Her eyes held a hint of mischief and vast wisdom. A spirit who roamed two Realms for over fifty years had much knowledge to impart. Anaya always appreciated gaining a deeper understanding of the Spirit Realm; it fascinated her. From Anaya's estimation, Beatriz had been around fifty when she died, as her tan skin was wrinkled in some areas, but she was still very pretty. The blue tattered dress and shawl told Anaya that Beatriz had spent most of her life in poverty. Her small hands were weathered from rough work and hardship. Beatriz had suffered a sudden death; she did not have the physical look of a person who had suffered a long illness. Her body was pear-shaped and curvy, the traditional build of women in Mexico. Anaya opened her eyes and looked over at Emma with wonder.

Anaya felt her daughter's emotional shift, and opened her eyes. "It's amazing, isn't it?"

"I hear her speaking. She's telling me all about her children. Can you hear her, too? She speaks Mayan. She is asking me specifics about Daniela."

"No, I don't hear her. She's your spirit. Remind Beatriz we need as much information, as quickly as possible. Show her in your mind where she needs to go."

Emma closed her eyes again and joined minds with Beatriz, who mapped the way. She started with the last place Daniela went: Beverwyck Park.

15

"I CAN'T SWING DANCE!" DANIELA looked at Daphne in panic. The cab had dropped them off at the Greenwich Village Inn. According to the cabbie, it was the largest dance hall in the city, and was filled wall to wall with people dancing and socializing. Daniela felt way underdressed and out of place, even if Daphne swore they looked "tossed to the bricks," Daphne code for looking good. Daphne even insisted that Daniela use the product she purchased called "hair groom." The label claimed to tame obstinate and unruly hair. With the moisture in the air, Daniela's wavy and frizzy strands started to take on a life of their own. Had she known, she would have hung herself with a flat iron. Now, she just had the gunk to rely on.

The Inn allowed colored people inside who were light-skinned. Daniela passed the color test at the door. No DNA test, just a brown paper bag placed next to her hand.

"Good grief! They have alcohol here. It's illegal, you know." Daphne looked over at Daniela, trying to ignore her apparent distress. "Daniela, you look quite handsome."

Daphne adjusted her outfit. Daniela had picked out the gown, helped her dress—tying the corset a little tighter than was comfortable—and selected the accessories to complement it all.

"Thank you, Daphne." Daniela felt like punching the jerkoff with his stupid bag. She took a breath and calmed down. "You look quite elegant yourself, and no one is going to question your age with boobs like that. Now, stay close to me."

She felt suddenly thankful she had refused to wear the underwear that trailed down to her ankles like some base-layer. *What the hell was that?*

People in 1923 wore way too much clothing for her taste. A fashion victim walked past her leaving the stench of sweat deep in her sinuses—no deodorant and people layered in wool, twill, and velvet.

Yuck!

This little shopping spree meant the money would run out run out even faster, and Daniela hoped this Lainbites would pay for everything tonight. Meeting a hot guy in a public place had been her idea, but he was the one who chose this high-end club.

She discreetly sent him a text. Within a minute, a very handsome man approached. He was over six feet tall, with deep blue eyes and sandy blond hair. Flawless, really. He was well-dressed and elegant, almost regal in appearance. Although he was wonderful to look at, something inside of Daniela warned her to proceed with caution. Maybe because Jack had been attractive, too, or maybe just some stupid association she was making.

"I had hoped to meet two girls...?" he asked with a smile.

"We are," Daniela answered.

"Sweet. The suit works for me." He smiled again, then stared at Daphne. "I'm Lain. I got us a table by the band."

He extended his hand to Daphne. She gladly took it. She seemed mesmerized by Lain. Daniela felt a slight girl boner for him, no doubt, but he also gave her all kinds of bad vibes. She had the instinct to protect Daphne, and followed close behind.

"I hope you girls dance."

Daphne giggled with every word. She began chatting it up with Lain like they were old friends. Daniela couldn't hear their conversation over all the noise.

The band played wonderful jazz music, and every seat emptied as people flooded the floor. The women danced freely and sensually. Some wore short dresses that flapped as they moved.

Daniela smiled in awe as the reality of being back in time hit her again. She remembered seeing swing dance in really old videos and felt the same amazement tonight. These women, who would one day be grandmas, danced like they would never grow old.

Lain took Daphne by the hand and encouraged her to dance as Daniela took a seat at the table. She smiled at Daphne, who shyly copied Lain's dance moves. A mixture of swagger and suave, and the best looking man in the place. He was also the tallest by a land-slide, Daniela noted, as she stretched her neck to look around. It was surprising to witness how short people were in person back in the day, like she had landed in Munchkinland or something.

"Not up for dancing yet?" Lain asked as he and Daphne sat down.

"Not quite. I need some courage first." Daniela smiled.

Lain gestured for the waiter to bring them some drinks. "Daphne says you gals are from Jersey. Country critters out for the night, then?" He flashed Daniela a brilliant smile. An aura of mystery surrounded him. Looking at Lain was like staring out over the ocean on a clear day—it's beautiful, but beyond that there's an intrinsic awareness of a vast unknown world beneath the surface.

"Yes. Just visiting. Mr. Lain, where are you from?" Daniela smiled back. Her mother always warned "guy talk" was her kryptonite. With the way he stared at her, she could easily become mesmerized and want to go for a swim in those blue eyes. They seemed to swirl hypnotically. She needed to remain guarded.

"Well, I'm out of sorts with the Realms. So I've been in New York for a time, until things cool down. I was excited to get your picture. I didn't know they were allowing travel here again." Lain looked at Daphne. "She's a little young. Very beautiful. A great cover, for sure. You don't seem like the type to have been banished from the Realms." He turned and looked at Daniela again.

Daniela had no idea what he meant by Realms, banishment, cover, or travel. She looked over at Daphne to make sure she had heard him correctly, in case it was more '20s talk, but Daphne looked puzzled too.

The drinks arrived, carelessly dropped on the table by a stumbling waiter. The tall highball glasses resembled iced tea, but one sip assured it was whisky. A young man came over and asked Daphne for a dance. Daniela gave her a little shove to go. She was still pondering Lain's words, feeling it was best to talk less and listen more.

16

"YEAH, WE JUST NEEDED A little R&R," Daniela said.

"Yeah, I hear you. Although these people are super lowbrow, it's better than the nonsense in the Realms." Lain sighed. "I can't stand it sometimes. What can you do?"

"Right. For sure." She wanted to ask more about these "Realms," but felt unsure of how to proceed. Could he mean realms of time?

"So, Daphne told me where you're staying. Slumming it, no?" Lain laughed. "Probably just want to get the full experience with the bottom dwellers." A blaring trumpet made it hard to hear. Daniela scooted her chair closer.

"Yeah, we're a little low on cash. But it's okay. The rooms are always clean." Her voice fought with the big band, "The roaring '20s for sure, huh?"

Lain smiled and downed his drink and gestured for more. "These idiots. Can you imagine making alcohol illegal? Jeez, these cavemen need about 300 more years to evolve." Lain laughed at his own joke.

It occurred to Daniela in that moment that he knew she was not like everyone else. She felt like she had missed a punch line.

"So, Daniela, what's your last name?"

"Delgado."

Lain choked on his drink.

Daniela didn't see the harm in telling him her last name, but his reaction had her curiosity way piqued.

"Whoa, you're a bit far from your coven. How did you pull that off?" Lain cleared his throat and took another swig, finishing his drink. He looked at her with sudden unease, wiping his mouth with the back of his hand and studying her closely.

"You know my family? How?" her voice raised three octaves as her excitement got the better of her.

"Everyone knows your family. How can you be low on cash?" He laughed again, as if the thought was completely preposterous. "Look—there are only a few of us around, so don't snitch. If you're low on cash, I can help you out." He squeezed her thigh under the table. "You seem like the type that doesn't follow the rules anyway."

His hand slid farther up and grazed the zipper of her pants. Daniela didn't move; she had to play it cool.

"No doubt. Snitches get stitches." She took a swig of the whiskey. "I'd appreciate your help." Then gave him a slow smile, and rose to remove her blazer and rolled up her shirtsleeve, exposing a small glimpse of her tattoos. Long underwear or not, her body started to sweat, plus she had to move to get his hand off her crotch.

He seemed very pleased with a peek at some skin.

"You're crazy and beautiful—my favorite combination." Lain's eyes traced every part of her, as Daniela took her seat again. "Be careful with your art around these buffoons. They tend to be highly intolerant."

"Point taken. Any other suggestions? I want to make my visit as pleasant as possible."

Daphne sat down next to them again, her cheeks a crimson red. She gulped down some alcohol while Lain watched her intently.

"Daphne is too young; she could easily get hurt. Best send her home if you want to hang out with me and my friends," Lain suggested.

Daphne gave Lain a hard glare. "I'm not leaving Daniela for a second, so just forget it!" Daphne looked over at Daniela. "Tell him."

Daniela felt tempted. She wanted to know more about this man. He seemed full of secrets; critically important if she ever wanted to get home. He also seemed to know a bit about her family. He said he was just visiting, which might mean he could go home, and possibly tell her how she could, too. He had no restraint about her color or the cross-dressing. He appeared as accepting as a person from her time would be. Her mind swirled with possibilities.

"Tell me, Lain, what exactly do you know about my family?" Daniela saw no point in playing games. She needed information. The thought of looking for any relatives had not occurred to her.

"What's it worth to you, baby doll?" Lain gave her a look that dared her to stop him as he again moved his hand up her thigh.

"I told you, I'm pretty cash-poor right now." She grabbed his hand under the table and firmly removed it, "but not that poor." Then she winked at him.

He laughed and gestured for another drink. "I'll give you some cash to tide you over, but you have to promise to come out with me again. It's been a while since I've come into new friends." Lain looked like he was thinking about how much to say; perhaps he felt tested. "Everyone knows Anaya. She's not a fan of mine, though. Seems she felt I was a bit of an asshole in our last dealings, and the tab is still running. I would appreciate a good word from you."

That was her grandmother's name: Anaya Delgado. Daniela could not remember how old she was in 2030. Surely not old enough to have a conversation with Lain in 1923. She'd be over one hundred, and she'd have to be a fetus right now. Daniela did the math in her mind again. It did not add up. Even though she never knew her grandmother's exact age, she barely looked over fifty. People always commented and said Anaya and Emma looked like sisters. Daniela decided to take a chance, in case it was a great-great-grandmother of whom he spoke.

"Anaya Delgado doesn't take orders from anyone. She's a commander. A good word means nothing, unless it comes from her directly." Daniela smiled. She hoped it came off convincing. That's how Mom always described Anaya, but Daniela knew the soft side of her grandmother. Even if they had grown distant with school, friends, and the everyday, she remained an important part of her life. "And never break a promise you make to Anaya; number one rule." Repeating her mother's mantra.

"Amen! You summed her up perfectly. She wants to turn my balls into bacon. A word from you might—so who are you, anyway, her niece or something? I'm trying to remember which one of her sisters has kids. Sabine didn't mention anything, last I saw her."

The color in Daniela's face drained. The drunk waiter came over (perfect timing) and dropped off more drinks, giving her a chance to regain some composure. Lain did know her family. But how could he know Sabine? And, if her family knew Lain, she would have known about it, surely.

"What's wrong? Did I say something to upset you?"

"How do you know Sabine?" Daniela felt like her stomach was dropping. She had that surreal feeling again, like she was awake but dreaming. "Well?"

"I know she just joined the coven. Everyone knows she's training with Anaya. Was that a secret or something?"

"No, you're right. I'm sorry. It's just...we're very private." Daniela tried to cover her reaction and kept telling herself to stay cool.

The word "coven" sounded strange to her. It made it sound like her grandmother was a witch or part of some cult.

"Yes, of course. So, girls, you want to go back to my place?" Lain draped his arm around Daphne and gave her a squeeze. It helped to lighten the sudden mood shift, however inappropriate.

Daniela wanted to ask him what year he had traveled from but couldn't form an articulate sentence to express all that she needed to about how she came to be in 1923. He appeared ready to leave and rose from his seat. Daphne eagerly followed. Daniela had to relax and find a way to confirm her suspicion.

"Maybe. Let's see what kind of phone you're rockin." Daniela gave him a smirk. She needed to see it, confirm that she wasn't crazy. If he had a phone from her time then he was like her.

"Okay, a quick flash. We don't want these cave dwellers to get any ideas." He slid the phone out of his front pocket.

It looked like an older model phone her mom had when Daniela was a kid. She remembered it because she dropped it in the toilet when she was three. She recalled her mother going crazy, since it had been new.

Daniela pointed and laughed; she couldn't help it. "Wow, who's the cave dweller now? Let me bring you up to speed, Neanderthal." She gave him a quick flash of her phone.

His eyes widened and he sat back down, pushing Daphne back into her seat. "Holy shit! That's some fine tech you have there. You have to come home with me now and show me the ropes on that thing." Lain's excitement was palpable. He went from cool to kid-like in a flash.

She put it away

He frowned.

"Next time, baby. We gotta roll. How about that cash?" Daniela hoped he would be true to his word about giving her some money.

"Honey, you are a mindfuck. I can't wait to see you again." Lain stood up and extended his hand to Daphne, helped her up. Daniela rose and followed them out the door. Despite the carefree atmosphere, Daniela could not hold Daphne's hand or in any way presume to be familiar with her. She followed closely behind, still protective.

By the entrance, Lain pulled Daniela aside. "Cash or check?" he whispered in her ear, making the tiny hairs along her neck stand on end.

"Cash." Daniela suppressed the shiver coursing through her body.

"Naughty girl." He placed a large bundle of bills bound by rubber bands into her pocket. It was a thick gangster's roll that made her pants bulge. "No kissing here. This isn't Harlem." He lingered by her neck again.

"Good-looking and rich—my favorite combination," she teased as she backed away a bit. Daniela knew "too close for comfort" would attract attention in a matter of seconds.

"Tomorrow night I'm taking you both to dinner. I'll have more for you then."

He walked out and hailed them a cab. As it pulled up, Lain turned and focused his gaze on just Daniela. She tried to discreetly adjust the bulge in her pants, as she had seen other men do.

Lain laughed, then told the cab driver where to take them, and paid the man in advance. "My meal." He said to Daphne. Then kissed her hand and opened the door for her. "Until tomorrow night."

She giggled, and then slid her dreamy smile into the back of the cab.

"Thank you, Lain. I'll let Anaya know you have been most gracious." Daniela gave him a firm, manly handshake. Lain held her hand for a moment longer than appropriate. He gently rubbed his fingers over her hand. Daniela couldn't help but let him, swimming again in his blue eyes.

And then he released her and took a slow step back.

Once the girls were inside the cab, Lain tapped the roof to signal the driver to take them directly home.

As they drove off, Daniela's mind darted around a million thoughts at once. She couldn't focus on any of them; Daphne's gushing was distracting. She chattered on and on about Lain. Daphne was too young and innocent to notice they were dealing with a shrewd shark, not a gentile gentleman.

"Let's talk about something else," Daniela finally interrupted. "What's naughty about saying "cash" when someone asks if you want cash or check?"

"You see, I told you!" Daphne all but yelled her favorite saying. "You just needed to get out to feel better. Look at you, ready to kiss some guy we just met. We can *tawk* about that."

Daniela noticed Daphne's accent became more pronounced with the alcohol. She seemed amused about being right again. Daphne reached over and hugged Daniela, teasing and tickling her, calling her a flapper and trying to make her laugh.

"Enough, Daphne."

The cab driver could see them. No place was safe.

Daphne needed to be aware of that at all times.

Daphne sat back, content nonetheless, and started humming an Alicia Keys song they had listened to earlier.

Daniela had started her slowly with hip-hop and pop. Daphne enjoyed the modern music. It was quite different from the orchestra music she was used to listening to. Daniela noticed Daphne's cheeks still flushed.

"Daphne Marie Buckley, are you drunk? I can't take you anywhere," she whispered playfully.

Once home, the bundle of cash amounted to five thousand dollars.

"It's the most money I have ever seen in my entire life," Daphne said, slurring. "I would marry Lain if I could. This is enough money to buy a house, Daniela! You see, I told you! Good gracious, he was gorgeous. One of us has to marry him." She finally collapsed on the bed, on top of all the money.

Daniela laughed for a moment. Only a girl from the 1920s would think of marriage so young. Her worry only increased as she looked at the money. What kind of dealing had her family had with this man? From what she read in the paper, Daphne was right—that kind of money could purchase an entire house —and a big one.

The talk of Anaya and Sabine left Daniela restless and full of questions.

Before she went to bed, a text came in from Lain. *Thinking of you, Daniela Delgado. How come no one knows who you are?*

Daniela wisely decided that less was more. She responded: *Private.*

LAIN LOOKED AT HIS PHONE. The last message not nearly enough to satisfy his curiosity. He didn't know where or how Daniela had gotten the tech she had flashed him, or how she had connected to his network. A rogue witch in New York City, away from the safety of her coven; definitely not something to be brushed off. Worse, she was a witch no one knew about. There was no way Anaya would allow one of her own to roam about unprotected, or with a human.

All of his informants had come up empty. With the exception of the flyer his man handed him, there was very little available. Only three things were certain: Daniela needed money, she was on the run, and she appeared to know nothing about him. Any immortal banished from the Realms and sent to survive on earth automatically feared him. He was known as a monster. Daniela seemed to *almost* like him, a drastic contradiction to what he was used to.

The immortals like him had lived on earth hundreds of years ago, until they discovered ways to manipulate magnetic fields to unlock portals and eventually roam and inhabit the five Realms. The majority left earth, preferring to live apart from humans. When an immortal arrived on Earth, there was no protection—unless one paid dearly for it.

The Santa Muerte Coven was the only coven of immortal witches tasked with protecting the Earth and keeping it a viable planet for all. The leader of the coven for hundreds of years and counting: Anaya Delgado—a powerful witch who ruled with an iron fist. The witches who worked with her abided by a strict code of service; it meant no nonsense, and Daniela sure had it right when she described her.

According to Lain's sources, Anaya remained unable to leave the coven home and relied on her subjects to carry out various jobs for her. All her power fed from the Earth under her feet, and the spot where the home was built hid a treasure trove of secrets. The more witches in her coven, the more powerful they became. The longstanding rumor was once Anaya had a successor to lead the coven, she would be able to leave her home and her job as protector. *Perhaps Daniela is on the run from such a permanent position, if she really is related to Anaya.*

No one wanted that job; dealing with humans and the immortals was a no-win situation. How Anaya had lasted for over 300 years was anyone's guess. Lain also learned from his spies that Sabine was training closely with Anaya, and perhaps would become her successor. But Daniela presented a wrinkle in that plan.

His hunch said there could be more amiss. Daniela showing up out of nowhere could not be good for him or his business.

How did she have that technology? It appeared far more advanced than his own, and it had taken quite a bit of work to create the phone he had. He and his engineers worked tirelessly to successfully incorporate the technology they used in the Realms on Earth. A relentless and daunting task; humans were a century behind the Northern Realm. The whole planet had to be "wired for sound" so to speak. It took nearly a decade to get it all synchronized. Now Daniela shows up, out of thin air, with her fancy gadget. Maybe she's luring Lain into a trap that's been fashioned by Anaya? No way would he become chitlins for her.

He stood outside the boarding home where the girls were staying, thinking. He folded up the flyer and placed it in his pocket; it might come in handy.

To his surprise, the place was not warded, a common and customary practice. He should have been thrown at least fifty feet in the air by a basic ward, but nothing happened. This further confirmed his suspicion—he could manage dealing with a young novice. But where was she from?

Or when?

His T'zi had been at the club, listening and observing. The ability to shift from human to wolf form was not the reason he was in

Lain's employment—it was the powerful telepathy he possessed. Tonight, Callen's mindreading picked up some strange story about time travel. With the witches, anything was possible.

He let himself inside and found the room they were in. He could smell Daniela from the door; earthy with lavender undertones. He liked it. Lain opened the unlocked door and entered the room silently.

He saw Daniela sleeping next to Daphne in the small bed. Her long, tan legs barely fit. She slept in strange undergarments, quite different from the long johns the humans wore. They were thin, small, didn't seem to serve much of a purpose, except allowing Lain to get a full view.

She was beautiful. Her torso was openly exposed, and she had a lean body with curves. To his surprise, she had ample breasts that wanted to spill out of the top that stubbornly restrained them. She had hid them well in the suit. The tattoo he glimpsed earlier ran up from her wrist to her shoulder, a display of intricate artwork with colors he had not seen used in over fifty years. He wanted to take his time exploring each pattern and all their mysterious details. His greedy eyes were hungry for more. He was developing an insatiable appetite for all things Daniela. Lain approached the bed, curious to touch her arm. Her skin looked soft, and he wondered if it would feel warm and supple. He pulled back in extreme disappointment when he saw a shadow in the corner move forward.

Interesting. Daniela had a spirit protector instead of wards. The spirit blasted him with a powerful draft of cold air, warning him not to touch her.

Daniela felt the strong draft and turned over in bed, reaching for the blankets. She snuggled closer to Daphne for warmth.

Lain moved around the bed and watched as the spirit followed him—a small woman in a blue dress. She removed her shawl and placed it on the floor.

He didn't need to close his eyes to see the woman on guard. She pointed to the door. He sensed she would ask nicely at first, but then all bets would be off. She glared at him, smugly daring him to challenge her. The sensation of cold crept into Lain, ran up his legs like the floor was suddenly made of ice. It actually felt like his legs were being encased—a rapid deep-freeze all the way to the bone.

He knew this spirit would not mess around, tiny or not. He darted from the room, unprepared for a showdown.

Tomorrow night, he would have time to probe the girls further, get rid of the spirit, and take the phone. As a bloodletter, he could handle the ghost and easily track her in the Spirit Realm.

DANIELA DREAMED ABOUT HER MOTHER Emma calling
for her. She could see her at the old house in Merida, at the trestle
dining room table with all the aunts, enjoying a grand feast. Daniela
noticed an empty seat next to her grandmother. The chair suddenly
erupted in fire, but no one else seemed to notice it. She ran up to
everyone and begged them to put out the fire. They ignored her. An
older woman that Daniela did not know walked her to the chair and
waved the fire away. Daniela sat down next to her grandmother and
held her hand. When she looked up, she noticed they were all holding hands.

The dream stayed with Daniela through most of the morning.
It felt like she had actually been there. It made her shiver. Who was
that older woman? She had never seen her before, but could recall
her face and the blue dress so clearly.

Daphne ate breakfast quietly. Daniela's plate of eggs grew cold,
her appetite apparently sated by worry.

"What's wrong?" Daphne raised an eyebrow.

"I want us to leave. Tonight. I need to go to Mexico and see for myself who Lain was talking about last night."

Daniela didn't want Daphne to be alone in the city, but if she chose to stay, then this sadly would be where they parted ways. She would leave her as much money as possible and take only what she needed for her passage.

"I feel anxious and restless, like I want to run outside and not stop until I reach Mexico. I can't stay here another moment. Everything inside me says I'll find the answers I need with my family."

"Oh, okay. Hang on a minute. How will we get there?" Daphne asked cautiously. "I can work on the arrangements after breakfast. I'm going with you." Daphne was firm in her decision. "And, frankly, I'm hurt you would consider leaving me."

Daniela felt frazzled and she wasn't sure if it had to do with Lain.

"Is this because of our new friend?"

"He's bad news, Daphne. Be very careful what you say to him...if we ever see him again." Daniela finally took a sip of her coffee.

"I like him. I think he could give us more information. He seemed to know a lot about your family. He knew a few of the people you showed me from the pictures on your phone. We don't know if he is a time traveler, or what else he knows. I say we work him over for more information."

Daniela laughed. "Work him over? And just how do you plan to do that?"

Daphne had certainly increased her vocabulary. Daniela had educated Daphne on the language her generation used—apparently too well. It was the cat's pajamas or the bee's knees according to Daphne, who had also taken the time teaching her the slang of 1923.

Daphne smiled coyly. "Not me. You. You see him tonight and get him tipsy. Get him to spill all he knows."

"Will you wait here?" Daniela asked, but already knew the answer.

"He said I was your cover. What do you think he meant? We meet him alone, not with any of his friends. The two of us can handle him if he gets out of line." Daphne nodded firmly—at least she agreed wholeheartedly with her own plan.

"Fine. I'll set it up." Daniela took out her phone and sent Lain a message.

His quick response surprised her: *If you are who you say you are, then you would know that I am nocturnal.*

Daniela read the text aloud.

Daphne gave her a curious expression. "Goodness gracious, he likes to play games. What a peach. Perhaps, respond in kind."

"Ah, you mean sarcasm with a sprinkle of 'who cares?' Yes, that always gets a guy's attention." Daniela smiled at Daphne, who was deep in thought, attempting to decipher what Daniela had just said.

I know who you are, and you would never miss an opportunity for a booty call. Daniela smiled, impressed with her own wit.

The response stopped her cold: *You have no idea who or what I am. Come nightfall—run.*

"Is this a threat?" Daphne asked. "Do you think he wants to hurt us? Why would he threaten us?"

Daniela felt a cold draft and hugged herself for warmth. With the cool air came a strong sense of unease. "We're not going to stay to find out," was all she could reply.

LAIN SMILED AS HE LOOKED at the phone. The half-wit didn't know she was already being tracked. His friend trailed in hot pursuit. He enjoyed a good game of cat and mouse. Lain needed to make sure this capture would be worth his while. He called Sabine, sure that she would take interest in an imposter using the coven name for self-gain. She hunted any rogue witches or practitioners of dark magic for the coven.

This will surely pique her appetite…and possibly get me back into the good graces of Anaya.

Lain continued to wonder about the amazing tech Daniela carried, a valuable acquisition that he would keep to himself. It would help his network and business dramatically.

Sabine finally answered her phone after his fourth attempt to reach her. Not surprising; his calls were never welcomed. Everyone regarded him as malicious, a rabid dog—and with good reason. Those who didn't—died.

Sabine, as expected, was very interested. She offered 100k for a capture. Chump change for the coven and a low-ball offer in Lain's mind, but a step in healing some bad blood and an opportunity to have a witch in his debt. A double-score for Lain, the guy who expected to always come out on top.

Sabine wanted to interrogate the girl. Lain was to keep her conscious. There was no bounty for the irrelevant human.

Easy enough.

THE GRACE LINE TOUR BOATS sailed from New York City Harbor to South America once a week. The advertisement in the *New York Times* promised a first-class voyage and a stop in the Yucatan. Luckily, it set sail the next day. Daphne booked their passage. Daniela had to ride in steerage, but getting to Mexico remained the priority. No need to ruin their last day in America with complaining. Daniela had come to grips with the way things were, but she remained hopeful things would be better in Mexico.

"You see, I told you," Daphne teased, flashing the tickets at Daniela as she approached.

"Yeah, yeah. I love you, too, you pain-in-the-ass-little-know-it-all." Daniela turned off her phone and put it in her suit pocket.

Daniela thought she'd better remain dressed as a man through their voyage, to prevent anyone from trying to hurt them. Two women travelling alone had disadvantages. She was fond of the suit Daphne had picked out and was getting used to all the layers, anyway—a unisex look for her time. Overall, it was better than a corset.

Daphne had tried to dress her as a girl, too, but Daniela just didn't fit the 1920s mold. Her height, tattoos, and even the way she walked gave away that something was amiss. Not to mention the hair....

They wanted to remain inconspicuous.

After a few hours of listening to music together in their small room, Daniela had cabin fever.

"Come on! Just a short walk."

They had a short stroll already that morning, to get the tickets, but that was hours ago. The opportunity to explore Manhattan became too tempting. Everything around them was under construction. Daniela tried to explain to Daphne how wonderful the city would become, where the Lincoln Tunnel would be dug and where the George Washington Bridge would be built. They noticed a boat where some men were filing people on board—it was for deportation. According to the man shouting next to them (the one throwing garbage at the boat), they were accused anarchists, and being sent back to Europe. There was an eerie similarity to 2030, but the magic word used to deport and mistreat people was "terrorist." The notion left Daniela with an uneasy feeling.

Just as people were being sent away, another boat arrived with new immigrants hopeful for a fresh start. Daniela and Daphne sat and people-watched as the new arrivals went through the inspection process, either being allowed or denied entry.

How awful, to have crossed an ocean only to be sent away, Daniela thought.

Yet, not much had changed in the last hundred years. Access to the American dream remained very costly and extremely limited. Daphne spotted a group of stowaways making a run for it. They cursed in Italian. Daniela laughed. They had grit and determination, an important reminder that she carried the same blood and spirit.

Daniela watched them disappear into the crowd with immigration officials close behind.

"People like that are the ones who make this country great. They probably have four generations in America by my time, just for making a run for it right now." Daniela smiled at Daphne, who was recovering from the scene. She did not look amused.

They decided to walk farther up.

That's when Daniela heard a man yelling. They turned around.

Roger ran at them. "Stop him! He has my daughter!"

Daphne's face paled as she grabbed Daniela's hand to outrun her father. Hanover Square, a congested area, full of people coming and going from all over the world. Dodging Mr. Buckley was difficult amid the crowd. With all the stowaway action, everyone jumped on alert, and people tried to block them from escaping. Roger started gaining. Many of the men standing around began running to help.

"Daniela, if he catches us, just go without me." Daphne began crying.

They stopped behind some crates to catch their breath. "Daniela, did you hear me?"

"Don't be silly. We can outrun him. You're not going home!" Daniela grabbed her face between her hands and gave her a kiss on the cheek. Losing Daphne was unthinkable at this point. Despite her trepidation that morning, they needed each other. "We just have to find a place to hide."

Daniela looked around.

A man ran by them, then backtracked. "He's coming. Come with me. I'll keep you safe."

He smiled at them as he extended his hand. The man was white and tall with handsome features.

Don't trust him, echoed a voice in Daniela's head. A cold shiver ran down her spine. Daniela could hear the crowd gaining. She had no time for the voices in her head. She looked at Daphne. She seemed hopeful the man could help them.

"Come on! There's a warehouse ahead. You can both hide there." He gestured again for them to follow.

Daniela swallowed. There were two of them. If he tried anything…it was one man versus that crowd…? She gave Daphne a look of understanding. She went with her odds—they would fight one man, if they had to.

As she grabbed Daphne's hand, she felt another cold draft and shivered. This man could be leading them into a trap.

Either way, it was over…. They followed the man as he led them to the warehouse. Once inside, the small windows near the ceiling were the only place for light to come in. This created a dark and moody space that didn't seem all that safe.

The man closed the door behind them, locking it. "Come on, follow me further in. No one will see you."

Daphne clung to Daniela's arm. She looked around. Large hooks hung on the walls. There were various tools and machinery all around. "Daniela, I think we'll be okay," Daphne tried to reassure her.

There were available weapons they could use, if they had to. Daniela rubbed her arm kindly. They had each other—that was all that mattered.

"Here. There are some chairs to sit and wait till the crowd dies down." The man gestured and displayed an easy smile. "I'm Callen."

"Why are you helping us?" Daniela asked.

The smile suddenly disappeared. "Lain sent me."

Daniela grabbed Daphne's arm and jumped in front of her, in an attempt to shield the girl from whatever was to come.

21

BEATRIZ COULD NOT RETURN TO tell Emma she had located Daniela, as planned. The girls were in too much danger for her to leave. Beatriz found Daniela to be a capricious young thing who lacked any insight into her own grave situation—not at all how Emma had described her. Beatriz studied them both carefully, learning a lot in her short time as Daniela's spirit guide. Daniela was easy to speak to through dreams, and she was definitely a witch like her mother. The only problem was Daniela didn't know it and she didn't pay nearly enough attention to what Beatriz tried to tell her. Spirits could communicate with the living through metaphors and suggestions in dreams.

The man who had visited them was not human or a witch, and both girls seemed oblivious to the ways of the worlds. Once in Mexico, they would be safe if the coven could recognize that the girl was one of them.

Beatriz could feel the pull of Emma's call, but she could not risk it. The man holding them in the warehouse was equally as dangerous as Lain.

Beatriz let a cold draft hit them all to alert them of her presence. Again. Callen scented her and took a step back from the girls. If Daniela passed out, then Beatriz could take over her body and get them out of their current predicament, and then make chicharon of this guy.

$$\dashv\vdash$$

"WE CAN DO THIS TWO ways, ladies. You decide." He looked around the warehouse, searching for something. "Now sit down and relax." He pointed to chairs. "Lain will be here in a few hours. I would hate for him to find you messed up. I prefer to deliver un-harmed."

With the way he stared at her, Daniela knew he was ready for any move she might make.

"Witches can never be trusted, but all I sense from you is fear and scattered plans of making a run for it."

"We have no dealings with Lain. We're on our way home, to Mexico. My grandmother is Anaya. She will be displeased to hear of our treatment."

Callen laughed. "Nice try. You say that so convincingly, like you truly believe it. My senses don't pick up lies, but witches are tricky.

The coven is paying us for this. Seems they have no clue about you. They certainly don't like all the name dropping you've been doing."

"I have proof! They don't know me yet, but believe me—I am her granddaughter." Daniela felt he could be swayed.

By his expression, he knew who Anaya was too. "The problem is the coven only wants you. Your human is really not anyone's concern." He growled at Daphne. "I will give you the chance to send her to the knuckle draggers outside, or she can share your fate."

Callen walked over to the one dirty window that was at eye-level, searching for the rabid crowd. He shook his head in disgust.

Daphne looked at Daniela, pleading with eyes that seemed to be filled with an animal panic. "I want to stay." She turned to Callen, "Please don't hurt us."

Callen double-timed it back to the girls and grabbed Daphne by the arm, and pulled her to him. "Wrong choice, sweetheart."

Daphne trembled in his grip. She screamed.

Torn between fight and flight, Daniela's heart thundered in her chest. She had been hit by Jack many times and knew she could take a punch, but this man seemed different. The more she looked at his face, the more she noticed subtle changes in his features. His eyes were intensely colored, his teeth seemed to protrude and elongate, and his body seemed to be getting bigger. She was sans plan....

A distinct cold draft swept through her again, this time from another direction. She didn't know what to do. But she stood up, as if the draft were directing her. She nudged Daphne—but just a touch, as Callen wasn't letting go. Then she faced Callen, waiting for him to hit her. She glanced downward for a brief moment to absorb the blow and gather her strength. When she looked back up, the woman in the blue dress, the one from her dream, appeared. Stunned, she blinked to refocus…and then the woman was gone.

Suddenly Daniela heard a whisper.

"Duerme, duerme, duerme." It was the word "sleep" over and over again.

How can I sleep at a time like this?

Daniela took a flimsy breath. "Let go of her! You're hurting her!" She raised her hands to grab Callen when the cold draft grew in strength, like a tornado. All the hanging tools jittered against the damp cement walls. Daniela took an instinctual step back and looked around to see where that wind kept coming from.

That's when all the tools took on a life of their own, swaying ominously from their hooks.

"Enough with your magic!" Callen released Daphne and lunged at Daniela, shoving her. "If you hit me, it's on, bitch!"

Then Callen stepped back and grabbed Daphne, again, using her like a human shield, or something….

"Let her go!" As the words left Daniela's mouth, all the tools flew off the walls and started striking Callen, one by one, taking turns.

That did the trick; he released Daphne. She sprinted to Daniela's side.

The tools kept striking him—sledgehammers, a pipe wrench, bow saws, coping saws, hacksaws, shovels. *What was this place?* The

equipment appeared possessed. Weirdly, what would kill most people—a sledgehammer to the head—didn't even drop Callen to his
knees. He just became angrier with each blow. He should have gone
unconscious by now from all the bleeding, but he fought on, en-
raged. After a while, he appeared to be winning. That's when he
lunged at Daniela again.

She ducked, a natural reaction, and so he caught Daphne by her
long hair. Daniela turned and jumped him. He punched her in the
face, then smacked Daphne. Before long, he had overpowered them
both. His rage and delight seemed to increase exponentially with
each blow he inflicted. The tools continued to bombard him, but at
this point, he was either numb, or immune to their effect.

Callen finally dropped Daphne like a ragdoll. She lay unmoving.
He slid over and grabbed Daniela, who was on her knees, attempting to rise. He kicked her in the back to flatten her, then flipped her
onto her back with a kick, straddled her, and wrapped his massive
hands around her delicate neck. He squeezed until the color in her
olive face changed to a pale white, and her lips turned blue.

That did it.

The tools dropped to the floor. The magic show was over folks.
Callen got off Daniela, gave Daphne a final nudge—nothing. Callen
reached in his coat pocket and pulled out his phone.

"Got 'em, Lain. Ready and waiting for you."

"Perfect. I'll be there within the hour."

Callen pulled up a chair and sat very still, trying to sense where the spirit went.

It was suddenly gone.

22

FINALLY, DANIELA WAS ASLEEP. BEATRIZ listened to Callen chat with Lain openly. She had about an hour. That was enough time to report to Emma. The pull of energy and psychic vibration she felt from Emma's call was stronger than her wish to stay. She would return and handle the situation. Daniela had many wounds to heal from and would be asleep for a while. The man had been ruthless toward the girls. Beatriz felt badly for him—she would be equally as vicious.

WHEN BEATRIZ ARRIVED IN MERIDA, Emma was kneeling before the altar. She had placed her offering around her and was now waiting patiently. Beatriz accepted the food, maize, and blood. The blood came from Emma, who had pierced herself through the tongue in the traditional way. Beatriz ate and enjoyed the offering.

Traveling to the future and fighting the Tz'i' exhausted her. This offering would give her the boost she needed to return and help Daniela. Spirits were not bound by time like the living, making Daniela's power a true rarity.

"Mija, what do you know about the man named Lain, and his friend, the Tz'i'?"

She showed Emma an image of them from her mind. As a witch, her power came from the Earth, so perhaps Emma had a connection to the men.

"Who are they? I know nothing about either of them. Do they have Daniela? Is she injured?"

"What do you know of the legends or stories of the Mayan people?"

"I'm American, Beatriz—I don't believe in fantasy or science fiction," Emma explained.

"Go and get your mother. I don't have much time. Make haste!" To Beatriz, Emma was Mexican and a Mayan; all the American talk meant nothing. The fact that she did not know about the legends, or either man—Lain or Callen—raised concern, but the elder witch had to know.

Emma hightailed it out of the room.

Beatriz searched her memory of the old stories. She knew Lain did not have to make an offering like this to speak to the dead. He was a bloodletter and Callen was connected to an animal totem, his spirit tied to the Tz'i', giving him the ability to transform into a wolf.

Nahuales, as they are called, are shape shifters who were nearly impossible to find, but did exist. Her meeting today confirmed it.

Beatriz continued to eat and enjoyed the offering as she mused about how Emma knew so little.

Emma entered with Anaya, who seemed pleasantly surprised to hear about Daniela's predicament.

"Ask the witch—she can confirm my story. She will know of the legends." Beatriz looked to Anaya, who nodded when Emma relayed the stories. Unlike her daughter, she seemed to understand exactly what was going on.

"Nahuales? Bloodletters? Time travel? This is madness! Total bullshit! Can you or can't you help me find my daughter?" Emma walked over and grabbed the cross with the intent to toss it in the fire.

Beatriz felt her heart sink. The careless way Emma held the cross was devastating and unnerving. How could someone so ignorant have gotten her hands on something so valuable? Beatriz glared at Anaya. It was obvious the witch had kept her daughter in the dark on purpose. Now Beatriz had gotten entangled in the game.

"No—please! I have done as you asked," Beatriz pleaded. "I will go back and keep her safe. She is in another time, trapped until your mother can help her cross over. She does not know what she is. I must know everything about her abilities. If not, she may be lost or killed by those creatures."

Beatriz looked from Emma to Anaya, waiting for one of them to speak and finally give her all the information she would need.

Anaya grabbed the cross from Emma's hand. "It's true, Emma—there are things that you do not know about the world you live in. There are details you chose to ignore about me, and this is your awakening."

"I want my daughter! I don't care about any of this! I'm wasting time here. I trusted you, but it's always more madness and crazy talk. I'm leaving." Emma pushed past her mother.

"Coven! Convene with me. It is time to show her." Anaya held Emma by the shoulders at the door.

One by one, her aunts filled the room. "Valencia is also nahual. Enlighten her, sister."

Valencia stumbled forward and adjusted her glasses. Emma stared at her in disbelief.

"There is little Valencia would convince me of, other than the fact that she's half blind. She can barely see anything in front of her. Just leave her alone, Mom."

Anaya scowled. "To you, she is an awkward hermit who is lazy and never around during the day. Watch and learn."

Emma watched with skepticism as her aunt transformed. The air in the ancient prayer room seemed to swirl around Valencia. Her eyes began to change from ordinary brown to iridescent amber, glowing like halogen headlights. Her body transformed, expanding with a display of tearing, rupturing skin, and snapping bones as she molded herself into the largest owl Emma had ever seen. It spun its head backwards and let out a hoot so loud the room shook. Nearby glass and ceramic was blown asunder.

Emma's hands shot up, covering her ears instinctually, but then just as quickly, she crumbled to the floor, passed out from the shock of it all.

Anaya had the twins move Emma to the spare room. It seemed everyone understood that Daniela's situation with Lain in 1923 was perilous. Before going back to the young, clueless witch, Beatriz received her instructions, too.

Then Anaya turned to her sister. "Valencia," Anaya commanded with a predatory conviction, "Go find Lain and bring him to me. It's time to finally crush his soul and send him to Hell."

This woman meant business, Beatriz thought, as she sailed out of 2030 Merida and back to 1923 New York.

LAIN ARRIVED AT THE WAREHOUSE, displeased to find the girls so badly beaten. He had wanted to do it himself. The pleasure he would have derived from each hit would have sustained him for a month. His kind luxuriated in causing pain and snatching blood.

"What will you do with the human?" Callen was looking at Daphne with a curious expression.

"Dispose of her. Why?" Lain asked.

"I could take her off your hands. She could be a breeder for us. She had fine features, and could probably survive a few births." Callen appeared eager.

"Why do you really want her?" Lain knew humans could barely bear their own children. Having a nahual would most likely kill her, if she even survived the mating.

"She's loyal, and a fighter—qualities highly prized for our kind."

Lain could tell he really wanted the girl; this became an open opportunity for Lain to benefit.

"Fine. Take her. I'll send you your fee. If she survives, she will owe me a debt…and so will you." Lain gave him a minute to consider the consequences of the deal. Callen said nothing.

Lain looked at Daniela, who lay unconscious on the floor. Lain allowed Callen to sense his sentiments. *This mistake will cost you dearly, Callen.*

Lain would keep him in his debt for as long as he needed. By taking the girl, Callen would ensure his servitude. No further words were needed. It was obvious in Callen's body language, he received the message. The T'zi' possessed a powerful gift—their intuition and perceptions were the strongest form of telepathy. This was the reason his kind was kept on Earth. The Realms contained well-guarded secrets.

Lain allowed Callen to read his thoughts of disappointment. Lain knew Callen did the girls a favor—if he had not beaten them, Lain would have done far worse. Lain had anticipated all kinds of torture, and now was stuck waiting for Sabine. He couldn't risk further damage. Callen saved the human's life and gave the witch a fighting chance.

"You owe me."

Callen gave him a nod and began to pick up Daphne off the floor. He understood there would be hell to pay. "There's something about the girl."

Lain looked at Callen intrigued. "It must be special for you to risk so much?"

143

"Perhaps." Callen hungrily slung the human over a shoulder and walked toward the door.

Stupid dog. He should have left her to die.

Once Callen left, Lain wanted to pounce on top of Daniela for so many reasons, but had to restrain himself. She was not regenerating from her wounds, and he did not dare inflict further damage. *Fuckin' Callen.*

He moved over to Daniela and began to undress her. He could still drink from her and was eager to find a place to pierce. Her blood smelled delectable. His mouth watered in anticipation. He continued to undress the many layers of her suit, carelessly littering the tool-covered floor with them. It had been a while since he had drunk from an immortal. Most who were on Earth no longer wanted to speak with the dead; they only cared about survival. Once Daniela was displayed in her undergarments, he paused.

"What do we have here?" To his delight, he found she had a metal ring protruding from her navel, along with two more on either side of her stomach. He smiled as he touched the steel ring. He slid his hand up her toned stomach and felt her breast.

Lain laughed loudly—both her nipples were pierced with the steel circles, too.

"You must be an angel sent from Heaven." A woman so ornately tattooed and pierced was truly a rare find. He ran his finger over her lips and fought the urge to kiss her mouth.

In his experience, only his kind went to such extravagance, believing it would curb blood lust. He wondered where else she was pierced, and slowly slid his hand back over her stomach, shivering as he felt the steel in her navel again. He was making his way down, praying there would be one more piercing when he heard Daniela moan. She sounded like a wounded animal.

For a moment, Lain felt his heart twist and flutter.

But that feeling went away when Daniela slammed her fist into his face.

BEATRIZ FELT THE SOFTEST OF touches trailing up Daniela's body. It seemed to tremble as it stopped on the stomach. She took the distraction as an opportunity to prepare her attack. She curled her fist and counted to ten.

Following the punch that launched Lain halfway across the room, Beatriz lept on top of him and kept them coming in double time. She beat the living piss out of Lain while chanting the various spells Anaya had instructed her to. They were most helpful. Within a few minutes, she had Lain bound with a chain and secured to a conveyor belt.

"You're not Daniela!" Lain spit blood from his mouth as he spoke. "I can tell from the eyes that Daniela is possessed. Are you the peasant woman who was in her room the other night?"

"I'm sorry. I don't speak English," Beatriz spoke in a Mayan dialect. She smiled, and ran her fingers through Daniela's hair; it was starting to curl. Beatriz examined Daniela's body with approval. She was quite strong, but would have eventually caved to Lain, like she had in the past to other men. Beatriz knew better than leave Daniela in charge.

Beatriz watched Lain, who was looking at Daniela's body with particular interest. The beast liked Daniela—appeared infatuated with her, even.

"You like?" Beatriz asked as she ran a hand down her body. Stopping at Daniela's breast, she gave it a squeeze.

He groaned in response.

Beatriz laughed at him. She enjoyed taunting Lain.

He pulled on the chains like a wild beast.

"Never! Never, for one like you." Beatriz spat in his face and slapped off the smirk that was brewing under the surface.

"What do you want? Why are you here?" Lain asked cautiously, as more blood dripped from his mouth.

This elicited further laughter from Beatriz.

"When is the witch coming?" Beatriz inquired and turned and walked around, searching for something...a metal pipe. *That should do it.*

That's when Lain noticed the back of Daniela's neck was also pierced. He bit his lip, stifling yet another groan. A fit punishment; he deserved this and worse. Lain promised himself that if her tongue was also pierced, it would be a sure sign that Daniela could be his mate. His reaction to her was stronger than anything he had ever felt.

"What is your plan with Daniela?" Beatriz demanded, turning back. She gingerly tossed the pipe back and forth. Daniela, when possessed by Beatriz, was turning out to be a real badass. The pipe finally rested in her left hand—because Beatriz was a lefty and wanted a good hit. "Speak, while you still can." She took a practice swing.

Lain didn't flinch.

"Ah, muy macho."

Lain responded in Mayan. "I will answer all of your questions. I just have to know if Daniela has a ring in her tongue."

The question seemed to puzzle Beatriz for a moment. She stuck her tongue out and showed him there was nothing there.

Lain breathed a sigh of relief. "Good. Now go fuck yourself!" he spat at Beatriz.

She laughed. "Look again, stupid guero," She lifted Daniela's tongue and exposed the barbells underneath and the other piercing under her top lip.

"Wait! Wait, goddammit!"

Before he could scream again, Beatriz beat him with the pipe. She took her time, ensuring he would never forget this moment.

LAIN AWOKE SOMETIME LATER, STICKY blood pooled up everywhere. He was missing everything—phone, keys, money, clothes. He was still chained to the conveyor belt, and despite the incredible pain, all he could think about was Daniela.

BEATRIZ STROLLED OUT OF THE warehouse without a care in the world, although with a little wear and tear from fighting, her new body quickly began to heal. She had Daniela and Daphne's belongings with her, along with a substantial amount of money she had swiped from Lain. She studied the two tickets for the boat to Mexico. Daniela was booked to ride steerage. Beatriz laughed and ripped them in half.

Going forward, Beatriz decided to change her name to Benito Ramirez, a tequila baron from Mexico who would travel in high style. She hailed a cab and showed the man the label inside Lain's silk-lined tweed coat. The man seemed to understand and drove her to the exclusive shop.

Once inside, she asked if anyone spoke Spanish.

A tailor came out from the back. "Ciao, Signore. Parlo solo Italiano."

"It's good enough. We all speak dollars." Beatriz laid out a large sum. The man was able to understand everything she wanted. Upon seeing the display of money, the shop owner promptly came out to greet her with food and wine, a service she was sure he reserved for his best customers.

She shared her story of traveling through New York City in search of the finest suits to take back to Mexico for important international business meetings. Beatriz relaxed on a lavish couch as the salesmen showed her all the latest arrivals. She delighted in the experience. The owner was all too happy to help. He offered to have his men drive the Baron to the boat, and ensured he'd be treated in the most excellent manner, as a man of his wealth was accustomed to.

"Excellent, my good man. When you come to Mexico, look for me—Benito Ramirez." Beatriz spoke in Spanish, laughing, and slapped the owner on the shoulder in a goodheartedly. She finished the fine wine.

Salesmen continued to trip over themselves to help Beatriz. At the end of her shopping extravaganza, she looked impressively polished.

Booking a room in a fine hotel was no problem at all. Beatriz walked into the lobby of the Hotel Biltmore like she owned it. Bellhops ran over with urgency to get all the packages her cabby needed to pass off. Her hypnotic smile and a few dollars, all that was needed to secure a room. Well, the three-hundred dollar suit helped, as well. After a luxurious bath and a New York strip steak, Beatriz fell fast asleep.

The shop owner did as promised and secured Beatriz a deluxe first-class cabin on the boat to Mexico. Food, champagne, and every other luxury were at her disposal when she arrived the next day.

Beatriz knew a little confidence went a long way. Daniela had none. She accepted anything she was dealt without complaint, even if it ruined her life or robbed her of choices. Beatriz wished she could impart even a fraction of her self-esteem to Daniela. She certainly had some to spare.

Beatriz waited for the maid to leave the cabin, then rested on the large bed. Once she fully relaxed, she left Daniela's body and let the girl rest. Beatriz sat at the end of the bed and placed her hands on Daniela's feet. She allowed the cold sensation to drift up Daniela's long legs and slowly awaken her.

"Wake, niña. Wake."

Daniela opened her eyes. She looked around scared and confused. She felt a chill encapsulate her feet and looked down.

Beatriz could tell Daniela recognized her from the dream, and perhaps the warehouse.

Daniela shifted back in the bed until she was sitting up.

"What do you want? Where am I?" Daniela scanned the room again. "Where's Daphne?" Her body started to shiver uncontrollably. Beatriz knew that was just anxiety. Daniela was probably remembering every awful detail. Beatriz noticed all the tiny hairs on Daniela's arm standing on end.

151

"Easy, my child. Your mother and grandmother sent me to look after you. I am Beatriz. You know me, right?" Beatriz spoke in a soothing voice.

"My…my mother?" Daniela's hand went to her heart again. "Did something happen to her?"

"They know you are lost in the past. They are helping you from the future. I am going to try to get you home. Do you understand?"

"No, I don't." Daniela trembled again. Her eyes welled with tears. "They know I'm not dead? Are they all right? I'm afraid to hope. Please tell me the truth. I can't take much more." Daniela cried and reached out to touch Beatriz.

Despite the tremendous energy needed to maintain a physical form, she felt Daniela needed it—to provide the child with some comfort. She extended her hand to Daniela.

"Emma and Anaya know you are not dead. They're working together to get you back where you belong." Beatriz rubbed Daniela's hair and then brought her up to speed.

"The child is gone. She had been taken by the other man by the time I returned."

Daniela needed a moment to grieve. The girls had become quite close.

"I think she lives. I did not see her spirit."

"She trusted me. I told her I would take care of her. I can't return until I find her."

"Your family wants you back as soon as possible. I don't think they will wait until you find the girl. It will be difficult enough just the two of us. Your grandmother has not told me how to get you back yet."

"When will you see them again?" Daniela asked, trying to control her emotions a bit.

"When they summon me, I go. I will tell them what you ask." Beatriz stood by the small window in the cabin. "You have a choice: allow me to take over and get you safely to Mexico, or stay awake and do it yourself. I will be with you, but can only warn you with cold and speak to you when we are alone." Beatriz turned. "Can you see me?"

Daniela nodded. She was still grappling with Daphne being gone, and she didn't have the strength to cope with it all, from what Beatriz could assess.

Beatriz changed to her usual spirit form. Daniela held her gaze.

"What will happen to me when you take over?"

"You can watch from inside and speak to me, here." Beatriz touched her forehead.

"Yes, take over. I can't…. Please help me." Tears streamed down Daniela's face as the cold engulfed her.

26

A HALF-NAKED AND BADLY BEATEN Lain was not the image Sabine wanted seared into her memory. Sabine reluctantly decided to help him, at least make him more comfortable by removing one of the chains and a lock that kept him secured to a conveyor belt, despite feeling disappointed with his failure to procure the witch. It was Sabine's chance, after so many years of being so low on the totem pole, to finally get into Anaya's good graces. Sabine kept the steel lock in her hand, slipping her middle finger through the shackle and dropping her hand out of view.

"Just my fucking luck, Lain. Now were both up shit's creek without a paddle."

"That little bitch got the better of me. She was possessed. That spirit with her is a piece of shit. I don't think Daniela would have been capable.... Daniela is submissive...."

"Sure as shit doesn't seem that way, Lain. She kicked your ass and left the carcass. Looks like she means business. You must have pissed her off real good. Weird. You're normally a charmer." Sabine looked at the last chain. She remained reluctant; trusting Lain was like finding a rabid dog and hoping it didn't bite. She had offered him the bounty to capture the witch; she thought maybe he lied about the whole thing in order to continue his feud with Anaya. But seeing him like this had Sabine thinking differently.

Lain stood with difficulty, swaying slightly, holding onto the conveyor belt for balance; his body still trying to regenerate from all the wounds.

"How did she get the better of you?" Sabine asked, trying to buy time while deciding what to do. Taking Lain to Anaya might be a better way to neutralize the constant threat he posed to the coven. "I've never you seen you in such bad shape."

Lain smiled. "She's quite beautiful. To be honest, I would let her get the better of me any day."

Sabine rolled her eyes. He had it bad for the witch. The girl managed to not only confine Lain, a feat the coven had been hoping to do for years, but also to beat the tar out of him. She must be quite powerful. Sabine's worry increased. Her priority was to keep the coven safe from any and all threats.

"Okay, from the beginning—tell me everything that happened. I need to track her, and fast. I can't let her escape."

Lain smiled again, a faraway look in his eye. "I counted at least eight piercings. Can you imagine, Sabine? What if she has more?"

God. Sabine took a seat near him in a seemingly casual way. "This is going to take a while." She started to loosen another chain, but kept a firm grasp on the padlock in her other hand. The machete

155

strapped to her pant leg was always within reach. She started to prepare in case this was a trap. She began chanting in her mind a spell
that would give her more strength. She was ready. She removed the
last chain. Lain continued to ramble about the girl's ass and her plan
to reach Anaya. Not good.

"So she's en route to Mexico. We can catch her at the port. How
much money did she steal from you?" Sabine hoped the topic of
finances would bring Lain back into sharp focus, and his attention
away from her hands.

"She took everything. About 20k in cash, my new suit, and a
gold necklace I was wearing. I'm in deep shit with regard to the
money, but I can't muster the energy to care," Lain laughed. "Either
way, I expect payment, Sabine." He paused and let the threat hang
in the air between them. "You will pay in cash, or with your life."
He smiled at her in a shameless way. "Unless the girl was a setup—
is that what this is?" His paranoia slipped into overdrive when he
caught a glimpse of her hand.

Sabine could hear her own heartbeat speed up. This was not
going to go well.

Lain's business was a combination of racketeering and extor-
tion. He used any immortals he could get his hands on. When they
were banished from the Realms and forced to live on Earth he
found a way to make them pay steep "protection fees." This kept
the coven overwhelmed by immortals seeking help to break away
from him. The rumor was that he used the immortals he "pro-
tected" to steal technology from the Realms and bring it to Earth.

Anaya had wanted to test his skills and requested some portable phones. The deal quickly went sour. He took her money and didn't deliver. She retaliated by taking some of his men. He only had a few months left to appease her or they would perish. Apart from currency and technology, he also collected blood debts as well. Immortals who fell prey to him were lost. They were at his mercy, and Lain was a savage. The capture of the rogue witch was a step toward healing the bad blood between Lain and Anaya. If he captured Sabine now, the coven would be weakened and at his mercy. The rogue witch would be a small disaster compared to whatever Lain had in store. Sabine couldn't let him get away. *God, why did I let him go?*

"Don't get stupid, Lain." Sabine kept a tight grip on the lock and continued chanting in her head. She felt her other hand ignite with magic. She slid her feet back and she gave herself a bit of space.

Lain moved fast attacking Sabine from the side. She punched him with the steel across the face and sent him staggering a few feet. When she reached for her machete, it was gone. Lain crept toward her, the machete in his hand.

He whizzed past her like a blur. She managed to evade the worst strikes, but took deep slashes all over her body nonetheless. One of her thighs got the worst of it. He was fast and deadly accurate, like a coiled snake.

Sabine stumbled backwards over a chain on the floor. She looked down, knowing she would not be able to reach for it before he attacked again. She needed some distance to hit him with the fireball that formed in her hand.

In a blink, Lain latched onto the other end of the chain and swung it, pummeling her against the back wall. It was the distance she needed. Sabine threw the fireball and watched as it detonated on his chest. She shot up and grabbed the chain from the floor, whirling it above her head and snapping it like a whip. It struck his body over and over. Meanwhile, her other hand was creating another fireball, she then moved forward, ready to ignite him again.

Despite Lain's wounds, he attacked once more. He charged her like an angry bull before she could light him up.

Sabine and Lain were now grappling like thugs. In the scuffle, Lain sliced the machete deep into her shoulder and twisted it, breaking the bone. He lowered his mouth greedily toward the wound to lick some blood. While he was momentarily distracted, Sabine reached her other arm toward a pipe on the floor. Once she touched the pipe, a surge of magic coursed though her fingers; then, in a jolt, it shot through her whole body. The pipe was still powerfully charged from the witch Daniela. Sabine hit Lain. He reacted like he knew that pipe well, quickly releasing her and backing away.

"Come on!" Sabine roared, goading him to keep fighting. The energy coursing through her made her feel invincible. The witch Daniela had cast a powerful spell on the pipe. Sabine could feel her body regenerating and strengthening with each second he hesitated.

She took another swing.

This time Lain leapt back before he got clubbed. "Fuck you, Sabine. Daniela will be mine. Your coven's days are numbered. She's more powerful than any of you, and will destroy you all!"

Then he vanished like a swirl of smoke into the night sky, leaving Sabine with a scorching hot fireball and no target.

He had to be lying. There was no way a witch this powerful would bother with Lain at all. He was nothing but trouble. Sabine needed to inform the coven. Her attempt to secure either threat had backfired. Anaya had been right when she called Sabine the Witch of Dual Disappointments, her nickname since joining the coven. Anaya was going to be furious. Sabine felt like she was constantly blowing any chance to become Anaya's successor.

Some days, Sabine just didn't know how she would keep herself going. She dusted herself off and strapped her machete back on her leg. She had to keep trying, no matter what. What was the alternative? On the bright side, she had all of eternity to get this right. On second thought, she wasn't so sure that was the bright side....

BEATRIZ "BENITO" RAMIREZ PROVIDED MUCH entertainment on board the boat. He had stories for everyone and spent outrageous sums of Lain's money on refreshments for his new friends. The alcohol flowed freely as soon as the ship hit open water. Daniela had decided to stay "asleep" until they arrived in Mexico and Beatriz was happy to oblige her. It took a few days to reach Vera Cruz, its busy port full of foreigners.

The boat docked. Being closer to the coven would provide Daniela with a well-needed boost of power and make it easier for her to digest the truth about her origin. Beatriz stepped onto Mexican soil and she felt the magic intensify and her body tingled all over. It made Beatriz feel like she was intoxicated, yet lucid. She felt wonderfully loose in all her joints. Being a witch from the Santa Muerte Coven certainly had its advantages. Beatriz was realizing that Daniela could be quite powerful. She was consumed by a sense of pride for the girl, like she was one of her own. Beatriz closed her eyes in an effort to accustom herself to her new reality. Then she allowed Daniela to regain control of her own body.

Daniela opened her eyes. She felt free and strong, almost confident. A rarity for her. Unaccustomed to feeling so good, she wanted to stop everything and question Beatriz, but the spirit was already on the move, several feet ahead. Vera Cruz resembled in some aspects what Daniela remembered from the future, with beautiful cobblestone streets and buildings. She was expecting to see a jungle, with thick vegetation and dirt roads. The city had a tramcar and more horse drawn carriages than New York, but the modernization was well underway with the plaza full of telephone and power lines.

She followed Beatriz, her own personal GPS, as they walked through the town and looked for lodging.

"We must secure transport to Merida," Beatriz called back to Daniela. "We are about 640 kilometers away. Perhaps a train or car."

Anything would be better than horseback, but would still be slower than what Daniela was accustomed to in the future. It would take several days to complete the journey. Daniela shuddered; she hated traveling through Mexico even in her own time. Her mother always scared her with stories about being robbed at gunpoint, but it would be worse now, without her. Her mom Emma knew how to handle any situation, and made her feel safe. Daniela looked over and saw Beatriz suddenly standing next to her. She was guiding her toward a cantina that had available rooms above the bar, and a sign in the window: "vacante." Not the Ritz-Carlton, but it would have to do.

Beatriz starting whispering instructions into Daniela's ear.

"Why are you whispering? You said you were a ghost, right? So they can't hear you."

"Yes, but if they see you talking to yourself, that might be a problem." Beatriz gave her a shove. "It is important for you, Daniela, to be considered a Spaniard and to act with an air of indifference towards the Mexicans."

"Why? Who cares?" Daniela was still trying to figure out if, as in America, racism and inequality was common in Mexico. She figured Beatriz knew best, and followed her directions.

"You! I need room—a clean one." Daniela spoke to the man behind the desk. She surprised herself with the volume of her voice and fought the urge to laugh. She had to treat him as people in America treated her. "Take up my bags, and tell your men not to steal anything."

Daniela's Spanish did not have an accent like Beatriz's. The man assumed she was a Spaniard and jumped at her command.

Daniela gave Beatriz a wink.

"Muy bien." Beatriz gave her another shove to follow her bags.

"Hurry, before they get stolen," Daniela snapped at the man gathering her bags.

"Right away, mi jefe." The clerk swiftly spoke to another man in a dialect Daniela did not understand. The indigenous Mexicans often spoke several languages.

Beatriz started laughing.

Daniela wondered, based on the looks the men exchanged, if she had become the butt of a joke. She adjusted her vest and glared. "Hurry up!" she ordered.

Once in her room, she began to unpack. A change of clothes and a quick bath were the only thing on her mind. She opened the door to the room and called out to a serving girl in the hall, to order some food. Colored or not, being a wealthy man in Mexico certainly had its benefits, Daniela noticed. She liked the way the staff jumped at every command and the way the women looked at her. It was restoring a self-esteem she had lost long before New York City circa 1923.

"Beatriz, what did they say, by the way?" Daniela watched her closely to gauge her expression.

Beatriz chuckled. "They called you a dog, and the clerk told the other man to go through your bags and bring him your best clothes. Also, to add water to all your food as a lesson for your arrogance."

"Shit! I'll be sick the whole time. Way to be passive-aggressive!" Daniela although starving, couldn't risk eating now. "For the love of Snoop Dogg, can I catch a fucking break?"

"You'll be praying for death if you eat any food here. They bring the water from the well. It's poison to the gringos." Beatriz seemed to delight in all this. "Mexican people smile and pretend to go along with the Spaniards and gringos, but underneath plot against them. Feelings are still hard, after the Revolution."

"What revolution?"

"The Mexican Revolution—didn't you ever hear of Pancho Villa?"

"Does that come with French fries? Then, no! Okay. I don't know a Pancho, and I don't know anything about a revolution." Daniela was angrily going through the trunk of clothes, trying to find something that would not make her sweat like a gorilla all day. It was 900 degrees in the little room. She walked over to the window and opened it, letting more hot air circulate into the stifling space. "This sucks!"

"There is so much you do not know. Mexico is in great turmoil and the sooner we leave Vera Cruz, the better."

"I don't know anything about Mexican history! I'm in a fucking hothouse, with no food or running water and a ghost. Excuse me if missed the class!" Daniela was definitely in the mood to throw a tantrum. A big one, like when she was little and would roll around on the carpet screaming. And she missed Daphne. That little pain in the ass would have had this all sorted out by now. Daphne had a way of making her feel better and encouraging her. Beatriz made her feel like an idiot. Daniela sat by the small window, smelling the horseshit below, thinking about everything and feeling overwhelmed. Her confidence boost slowly crumbling.

"So once we get to Merida, then what?"

"I don't know." Beatriz shrugged. "You convince your grandmother you are her granddaughter and ask her to send you home."

"Convince her? You think she won't believe me? Look at my face, I'm a spitting image of my mother." Then she realized... "Shit.

My grandmother doesn't know my mother yet." Daniela had always assumed her family would just automatically help her. "Why is everything so hard?"

"It's life, niña. Hurry up and change. I have much to teach you about your true nature, your heritage, and most importantly, your coven. You will feel better once you learn these things and the spells your grandmother wants you to. You will finally have an understanding of what you can do."

"Why was this all kept from me for so long?"

"Those are questions for your grandmother, niña."

DAPHNE AWOKE ON THE FLOOR of a dark cold cell to the sound of dripping water. Her left eye was badly swollen. Her head throbbed. She saw a tray of food that looked like it had been there for hours. She felt feverish and started trembling violently. The cold penetrated through her skin and deep into her bones. All she could smell was urine accompanied by a feeling of dread and doom.

The events of the last twenty-four hours hit her in a flash and she scurried to the corner of the cell. That man had terrified her. There was something not right about him. The sounds he had made and the way he attacked them. He was like some kind of wild animal.

Daphne bit her lip, trying not to cry. It hurt to take a deep breath, and she whimpered softly. She was so scared for Daniela. She knew nothing of what that monster might have done to her. She tried to piece together every detail she could remember, and then thought about her family, and started crying. There was nothing left for her. If she was to wait in this cell until she died, then all she could do was to accept her fate. Daphne thought that maybe a prayer might help her pull it together. She made the sign of the cross and launched into the Lord's Prayer. That's when a low growl echoed outside the cell. She pressed herself against the wall in the hopes of disappearing.

"There is no God here, girl. No sense in praying."

Callen was outside her cell. His voice amplified her trembling. It was hollow, sinister, and devoid of any emotion.

"I have been watching you sleep for an hour now. You're beautiful, young, and despite everything, still loyal to your friend Daniela. I sensed all your dreams and know more about you than you could ever imagine, Daphne. I know about your father, and all the filthy things he tried to do to you. The bastard has done more damage to you than you realize."

Daphne felt small in the cell. How could he know about her father? Was she talking in her sleep? She took in her surroundings trying to locate where Callen was standing. She could not make much out; every shadow, and there were a bunch, all looked like a monster. But she knew he was there, mocking her. He was right— she was not a virgin. Her father did terrible things, but she wasn't going to be ashamed. Daniela had told her it wasn't her fault. She had called it child abuse.

"I feel pity for you, Daphne. You are too innocent to understand all that was taken from you. At least in service to my father, your life will end honorably. Carrying a child for the king and staying in this cell is the most you can expect in your short life."

Daphne continued to search for him, straining her neck to look above the cell door.

"Eat, Daphne. You have been asleep for two days. Tell me what you like to eat and I will make sure it is brought down. You will remain in this cell, and, I, or one of the staff will see to your needs."

"Where is Daniela? I want to go with her." Daphne's voice was raspy, strained.

"Lain took her. She is most likely dead. Best forget about her." Callen walked to the cell door. He seemed to appear out of nowhere, startling her. "I will not hurt you anymore. I promise. What I did was to protect you from the same fate as your friend." Callen cringed as the words left his mouth.

"That's what my Da use to say. But he always hurt me, and I suspect you will too." Daphne wiped away tears. "If that's all you want to let me go, then let's just get it over with."

"You will stay in this cell until you are older, and then you will be asked to be with my father. If you accept, it could be that my father will take favor on you and allow you more liberties. No one will force you."

Callen wrapped his fingers around one of the jail cell bars; his hand was massive. This was way too close for Daphne's comfort. She pressed her back against the wall. He watched her in silence, like he was shuffling through the memories in her mind, deciding which he should dislodge and use against her next.

After a minute of deathlike stillness and silence, he finally spoke. "You don't believe me, and you think that suicide is the better option." Callen looked in the cell. He leaned down and took the small knife off the tray on the floor. "You will be guarded, and they will sense any plan way before you get a chance to do something stupid. I'll take this, so it doesn't tempt you."

Daphne cried futher. *How could he know?* "Please, I'm only a kid. Just let me go."

"You haven't been a kid since your mother died. But okay, honey—tell me what you would like. I can bring you some ice cream and cake after your meal."

Daphne could tell he was just playing with her. The evil glint in his eye gave him away. "Don't call me honey! You think some cake and ice cream will ever make up for what you're doing to me?" Daphne leaned down and threw the tray against the bars, splattering food all over Callen. "You eat it, sweetheart!"

Callen smirked. "I underestimated you."

"You have no idea!"

"I do, actually. I know everything that is going on inside that head of yours." Callen threw the tray Frisbee-style back at her, narrowly missing her head. "Sleep well."

Daphne listened as his footsteps grew faint. When she felt sure that he was gone, she slid herself over to the other side of the cell. There was a small metal cup of water on the floor. She gulped it down, wishing it was warm enough to soothe her raw throat. When she finished it, she saw another tray of food on the floor. It must have been the one from the day before. The food was hard and stale, but edible.

Callen claimed she had been asleep for two days. She felt it. Every muscle hurt as she dragged herself to a dirty blanket on the floor. Daphne gripped the wall and pulled herself up to stand. A wave of dizziness threatened to knock her over, she stood holding onto the bars and wrapped the blanket around her.

"Good God. Where the hell am I?" She took a long look at her surroundings.

ROGER WAS STARING INTO DAPHNE'S empty room, a re-
cent evening habit of his. He never went in, but just stared at the
void. Everything seemed frozen. The life that was once inside the
room was gone, replaced by a stillness that wasn't quite death. Since
his return from New York without her, the farm was falling apart.
Thomas was doing all that he could to maintain things, but without
Roger's help, the farm would fail and they would soon be left with
nothing.

Anger rose in Roger's body. He was disgusted with himself for
helping Danny. He should have left the boy to rot, or killed him. All
of this would have been avoided. Had he understood then all that
his new friends were teaching him about Negros and foreigners, he
would have handled the situation differently. Now, the large oak on
his property was being used for lynching and hanging. His member-
ship and position with the Ku Klux Klan was the only good that
had come from the loss of his daughter.

The meeting scheduled with the Klan tonight would include some financial supporters from a group called Watchers. They shared similar beliefs and would speak about the future, and how they could help each other become powerful organizations.

Roger's anger was eased with knowing the Klan had plans to help him. They promised a resolution for his daughter. The sanctity of his home and Daphne's white womanhood would be restored. He shut the door to Daphne's room and walked down the hall to his own bedroom to prepare for the meeting. Perhaps with the Klan's help, he would be able to save his farm as well. He would serve them with total loyalty. He had done worse in war and come back to nothing; now, his service would be rewarded.

Roger laid out his white robe, with its red insignia surrounding a white cross. It gave him a sense of pride as he looked at it. It made him feel useful, capable of restoring his family and helping his country. Roger knew all too well Thomas did not approve of the meetings or plans, but Roger understood there came a time when every man had to choose for himself—had to decide what they believed in, and whom they would chose to follow. Thomas would need to make that choice for himself sooner rather than later, too.

30

CALLEN ENJOYED WATCHING DAPHNE IN the cell, a nightly ritual he came to depend on. Her presence made him feel calmer. Most times, he would go to her in his wolf form, where her graceful hands would luxuriate in his fur. He enjoyed those moments. She was relaxed and even loving toward the wolf. They kept one another company. Callen was in his own cell, so to speak. Although free to walk the grounds, he was bound by his father's wishes and demands. His situation reminded him of Sisyphus, the Greek god condemned for eternity to repeatedly roll a boulder up a hill just to watch it roll back down, over and over. Callen's confinement also felt circular. This gave him time in perpetuity to master the task of pleasing his father. Yet, no matter how hard he tried, his brother Bren remained the light of their father's eyes. Callen was like the sand in them. Being second in line for the throne meant he was just an irritation to his father. Like Sisyphus, he had to rely on his craftiness and lies to work around the rules in the kingdom, often using his family's position to obtain what he wanted.

Once his father released him for the day from his mindless er-
rands and duties, Callen was free to sit with Daphne. She had beauty
beyond measure, especially for a human. Like her, he wished for
different circumstances. Perhaps it was the pathetic nature of the
humans that rubbed off on him—spending time with those less for-
tunate makes one feel good. He loved being with her. Because his
family would judge his feelings as irrational, Callen did everything
possible to shield his emotions.

Callen was on his back, allowing Daphne to pet his stomach. He
was falling asleep when his brother came in.

"Well, well, what do we have here?" Bren was holding a tray of
food as he approached the cell.

Callen growled and snarled, bearing his large fangs.

"Is this dog bothering you, my angel?"

Callen barked furiously at Bren.

"OUT!" Bren's voice boomed.

Callen scurried out.

DAPHNE WATCHED AS THE MAN who had shouted at the
dog unlocked the cell door and carefully set down the tray of food
on the rickety table inside the cell. Then he sat down, leaving the
door wide open. She knew she had to be careful, but was strangely
drawn to this man. After days of being in the cell with nothing, he

174

seemed to offer a bit of humanity. She couldn't help it; she imme-diately began regarding him as some kind of knight in shining armor in what was left of her rational mind. She barely blinked as her eyes darted from the man to the food, and back again.

"My name is Bren," he smiled.

His amber eyes sparkled with kindness. Daphne was sure she must look a bewildered mess. She prayed he wasn't there to hurt her—that she was perceiving the kindness in his eyes accurately.

"There, there, my little one. Come sit and eat, darling."

It was the way he looked at her, his soft demeanor, and the fresh food —Daphne felt her shoulders relax. She so badly wanted this nightmare to end.

Be careful; trusting a man never ends well. The voice or her subcon-scious echoed somewhere deep inside her. But it was so faint, and the smell of the food so intense.

Daphne was starving. She lunged at the chair opposite the man, dug in with both hands. The food was still warm; she was so grate-ful.

She'd remind herself to look up between bites.

The man looked concerned for her, seemed to be examining her intently. He kept both hands on the table, too, always visible. "When I heard about Callen having someone down here I was outraged to discover it was just a girl. I'm very sorry for the manner in which you have been treated."

Daphne nodded and continued to shove more food into her mouth, not caring about her appearance or the apology.

175

He continued to stare, as if trying to open a hole in her mind.

She swallowed quickly, fearing he would change his mind and take the tray away. Thankfully, he didn't, and they just sat in a companionable silence while she finished, his eyes remaining fixated.

The food felt like a stone in her stomach, she had gone days without eating. "I want to go home. Please." What she really wanted was to find Daniela. Her home was gone. She could never go back there and endure more abuse from her father. Daphne suddenly felt very tired and weak. What was she going to do?

"Who is Daniela? Why do you need to find her?" Bren asked.

Daphne was confused. Had she spoken aloud her thoughts about her father or Daniela?

"Your friend who saved you from your father. I sense great loyalty to her. What she did for you was noble."

Maybe I did, but when?

"Yes, she's my friend. I think she's in danger. We were separated when Callen attacked us in New York. We were on our way to Mexico so she could find her grandmother, Anaya."

"I'm intrigued with the story in your mind, about your friend, Daniela. You believe she was perhaps some kind of time traveler."

"I never said that."

"But you believe it, every word of it. You weren't just going to Mexico, you were going to find Anaya and the coven."

Daphne hesitated while her mind considered the possible reasons this man knew so much. Fear began to worm its way into her thoughts as an otherworldly conclusion formed. He wasn't like her and she knew from her memory at the warehouse that Callen wasn't human; he couldn't be.

"Luckily, you helped my people avoid a major diplomatic crisis. What you don't know is that your friend Daniela is a witch— if, in fact, she really is a relative of Anaya. Once the witches regain their own and they discover my brother's involvement, there's going to be hell to pay. But I'm hopeful that you can help me with that."

"How so…?" Daphne eyed the knife on the tray, silently praying she wouldn't need it.

Bren reached over and placed the knife in her hand.

"Keep it, if it will help you feel safe. I will ensure that you are returned, unharmed and well cared for. My brother's deviant dealings with Lain will not go unpunished. He will not harm you again. Hopefully, that will be enough to appease the witches and lessen the possibility of retaliation from Anaya."

"I don't want to stay here." Daphne uttered in a withering tone. She felt very weak. Like she had been dropped on her head, with no way to make sense of any of this. Bren rambled on, but he may as well have been speaking another language. Her mind felt full and the excess was now spilling out her ears. Daphne just wanted to sleep.

"The time travel stuff is something for the witches to sort out. They are always involved in something crazy, so I won't waste time debating if it's true or not. Getting and keeping my family out of conflict with Anaya and the coven is my top priority. Can you understand, Daphne?" Bren stood up and gently guided Daphne out of the chair. "Yes, you need to rest. This has all been too much for you. I will continue to explain it all. In time you will understand."

They began walking down a long hallway. Daphne kept a tight grip on her little knife.

The home appeared to be some sort of castle. Daphne could see servants scurrying about. One stopped and simply nodded at Bren, and then maneuvered cautiously around them.

"Your room is ready." He gestured toward a grand door. The gold knob and ornate carvings on the wood panels was something Daphne had never seen before. She imagined Bren and his family were quite wealthy to spend so lavishly on doorknobs and wood. Inside, there was a sizeable bed in the center of the room. The linens and décor were luxurious and the space was finely appointed with anything she could want or need.

"This is beautiful." Daphne wanted to sink her head into the pillows.

"This will be your private room. I gave orders to everyone that you are my special guest, to be treated with the utmost respect. If you have any problems, let me know immediately. I will take care of it."

"I'm scared of Callen. Is he here, too?" Daphne looked around, wildly. Her heart racing as she searched.

"Yes. He lives here too. You are under my protection now. I will deal with him. I hope in time to earn your trust. I will send word to Anaya that you are here. Perhaps Daniela made it back to the coven. I'll find out for you. Rest easy, now." Bren quietly turned and walked toward the door. "Get yourself settled. I will come check on you in a bit. You are free to roam the house as my guest. There are servants who can get you anything you need. Just ask."

The comment confirmed an understanding between them. The illusion of freedom for her cooperation was a start, at least. Daphne watched as Bren closed the door.

Her body shook with relief. Exhaustion moved in swiftly. The tattered soles of her shoes felt leaden as she inched her way toward the bed. Once seated, she began to cry. As badly as she needed it, sleep would not be coming soon.

31

"ANSWER THE FUCKING PHONE, EMMA…. I've been calling all week!"

Monica left another angry message. Her frustration increased with each passing day, making her feel scared and completely abandoned. Her mother-in-law's landline rang and rang, though she knew the house was full of people. Someone had to have heard it. What justification could there be for Emma not answering her phone? *Imagine if the police were to find Daniela—then what, Emma? Would your mother continue to be more important than us?* She stared at her Louis Vuitton luggage by the stairs. She had to stop this negative inner dialogue. It was crippling her. Monica took one last look around at the empty shell their home had become. Everything that mattered was gone.

How could Emma just leave her like this? How could Daniela just disappear with no word? Didn't either of them care about her? The cab to the airport would arrive any minute. Monica wiped the tears from her face and made sure her passport was in easy reach.

She wheeled her suitcase to the front door. *God, what was taking the cab so long?* Her impatience matched the irritation she felt about the whole situation. Finally the sound of a horn pulled Monica from her thoughts. *Ready or not, here I come.* She walked out and closed the door behind her.

"Hope you don't mind I cancelled your cab." Detective Hicks blocked her, but then extended his arm to grab her luggage. "I was able to get us seats together."

"I didn't know you were tracking me. Anything else I should know about?" Monica felt her face heat up, the anger boiling over. She wanted to let out all her frustration with Emma and scream at the detective. She didn't care anymore.

"Just that none of your calls have been answered. Not a good sign. Having company may be a good thing."

Monica shoved past him, not wanting to hear the truth. Having it in her head was one thing but the embarrassment of other people knowing was devastating. Confirming anything else was also out of the question.

"I understand why you're angry. You have reason to be." Hicks commented tartly. "I imagine Emma must have a good cause for the silence..." he hesitated for a moment, as if choosing his words carefully. "Although, nothing could justify what you're going through alone."

"It's her mother; you just don't understand." The tears spilled out again. "She's a controlling bitch, pardon my French, and is not fond of me in the least. She's keeping Emma away. I was never good enough for her daughter." Saying it out loud felt strangely liberating...and shitty at the same time.

Detective Hicks caught up with Monica and held the car door open for her. "After you." He handed her a tissue and seemed unaffected by the drama.

"Thank you. You're a gentleman. It will be helpful with Emma's mother—she a stickler for manners." Monica managed a smile. Perhaps having someone with her might be for the best. She felt unsteady and had not slept in days. Monica sat in the back seat and blew her nose. She went through her purse to find a mirror and grimaced at her reflection. At least she had some time to fix herself up before arriving in Mexico.

The ride to the airport went by in a blur. Hicks drove in a confident and sure manner, not rushed or hectic as Monica would have been if she had had to drive herself. Of course, that's why she had called a cab.... Monica kept quiet the entire ride as a sense of unease wrapped tight around her stomach. She had not seen her mother-in-law in many years. The last time had been the week before she and Emma were married. Emma had taken her to meet only Anaya. Monica was not invited to meet the aunts or uncles. Shame, she imagined. Anaya could never accept the union. Since then, she barely got a "hello" when Anaya called the house. Monica tolerated her rudeness for Emma's sake, but no more. Monica considered the possibilities of what could have happened had she insisted on being with Emma and Daniela seven years ago—on their last trip there.

The trip to Mexico was sudden, too. It started with that unfortunate camping trip with the Girl Scouts where Daniela had terrified everyone in the cabin with strange prognostications about demons, witches, ghosts, and even vampires. Monica had been sure it was some kind of psychotic episode or something. She had never seen Daniela in such a state. Not knowing what to do, they both slept in the car until Daniela could calm down. When they returned home, Daniela still struggled. After medication and therapy failed to help, Emma called Anaya who insisted on seeing Daniela for a spiritual cleansing. Anaya saw her, and said the "bad influences" were trying to take over. Monica was sure it was yet another dig at them—they were the "bad influences."

Daniela was cured; that's what Emma had said upon their return. At least she seemed to be back to normal when they returned, and had been ever since, or so they thought. This disappearance left Monica unsettled. Maybe Daniela had been hiding her symptoms all these years. Who knows what her crazy grandmother did or said to her. This was all Anaya's fault. It was at this moment that Monica was living with the regret of not going down there with them. She wished she'd fought harder. Even though this story was in the forefront of her thoughts these days—she couldn't shake it for some reason—she didn't want to share it with the police. The whole thing was crazy, and brought into question Daniela's mental health.

"You doing okay, Monica?" Hicks's eyes swept over her.

"Yeah, just zoned out for a bit." They were nearing the security line now. Geeshe, Monica barely remembered parking and getting out of the car. Hicks led her to the side, bypassing everyone else. He flashed his badge and they arrived quickly at their gate. At least that part was painless.

Before Monica knew it, she was in the air, looking out the window and trying to ignore the awkward silence between Detective Hicks and herself. She needed a drink.

"Sleep," Hicks suggested. "You look very tired, Monica. I'll wake you when we land."

"Yes, I just need a drink first—something strong." Monica leaned forward looking for the flight attendant. "Tell me, Detective, what's your name? Or do you prefer the formality?"

"By all means, call me Hicks." He offered his shoulder for Monica to sleep on.

Monica reassessed her prior notion of good company. She tried to relax and leaned her head toward the window instead. The flight attendant came back with the drink for Monica and a flirty smile.

When Hicks smiled back at the attendant, Monica noticed he had dimples. She supposed he was handsome, if one liked that sort of thing.

"Some pretzels too, Miss, if you don't mind." Monica said, interrupting their moment.

"Absolutely." The attendant winked at Monica.

Hicks rolled his eyes. He looked like he was about to say something when her pretzels were dropped off—but then changed his mind. Maybe he was an old fashioned, macho kind of guy who thought all women wanted him? Even a woman...who likes women. He was in for a rude surprise in Mexico. Emma said her mother and aunts saw little use for men. "Man haters" was the description Emma used for them. It made sense; none of them were married and the only men in the house were mutes. *Weirdos*.... How Emma's uncles had survived unscathed was a mystery. In fact, so much about her wife's family was cryptic. Having Hicks as an ally— and a witness to the numinous oddities they were sure to encounter in Merida—might be best after all. Maybe with Hicks there, they would all be on their best behavior. This was a gutsy move on her end, arriving unannounced and ready to take on the whole clan. Monica finished her drink, too tired to think anymore and slept, dreaming of Emma and Daniela.

32

MONICA AND HICKS STARED AT a large, empty lot in Merida. The exact location Monica had assured him they would find the house of Anaya Delgado.

"I told you, the house did not show up on a map. The address you have is incorrect."

"No. No! This is crazy. I've come here with Emma. There was a large house here, with iron gates. You had to have a code to enter. It was right here." Monica pointed to the empty lot in disbelief. "They couldn't have moved the entire house!" Monica started to pace. She fumbled around with her phone to call Emma again. Shit, it had been a long time since she was here. Maybe he was right.

"The address is wrong. Let's go back into town and see if anyone knows this Anaya Delgado. Try to calm down."

"Detective, the entire house is gone, for God's sake. This is crazy!" Monica was sure Emma would have told her if the family had moved. Nothing was making sense. She was aghast and embarrassed.

"It's all right, Monica." Hicks spoke with outward casualness, but Monica could sense he was fuming. "Come on, let's go into town and get some answers." He motioned for her to follow.

Monica wheeled her suitcase, huffing behind him.

Merida was a step back in time. It had large, baroque-style buildings and a church in the center of town that was at least four hundred years old. The cobblestone streets and large courtyard near the magnificent Catholic Cathedral bloomed with beautiful flowers. The place was full of merchants and tourists. Once in the town center, Hicks began to ask street vendors if they knew Anaya Delgado. All answered "no," but the expression on their faces told a different story.

"I sense they're scared to speak, or are acting out of protection of this lady. What does she do, anyway?"

They walked into a Silver shop. Everything was sterling, set with stones of turquoise, jade, and rose quartz. All handmade; it was stunning.

"She's a curandera—has been for many years."

The jeweler didn't cop to knowing anything about an "Anaya" either.

Hicks left the store. Monica gave the jeweler a dirty look, and followed. "I know he's lying," she whispered to Hicks when they got outside.

"Come on, let's eat something and regroup." Hicks began walking toward a tacos al pastor stand.

"I can't eat at a time like this," Monica's temper snapped.

"Relax, we have to blend in and observe." Hicks ordered two tacos from the vendor, then looked around the square carefully, trying to assess the situation.

As Hicks ate his tacos, a woman approached. She was petite, with wavy black hair, almond eyes. She had chains of gold draped about her neck. Monica quickly recognized the one necklace that had a large amethyst stone—an exact replica of a piece Emma always wore.

"Buenos dias, joven. Estan buscando una curandera?" She asked.

"Yes, we are. Do you know Anaya?" Monica asked, unable to take her eyes off the purple stone.

The woman smiled. "Yes, she is my sister. I am Lola."

Monica studied her carefully and exhaled with relief. "I've never met you, or the other aunts. I've only heard stories, but Emma told me you're her favorite. She speaks of you often." Emma had described Lola as "the nice one" to Monica many times.

"I'm Monica. Emma's wife, or as Anaya calls me, her friend…." Monica bit back a laugh.

"Yes, Anaya still refers to Emma's lifestyle as a friendship, yet everyone knows better." Lola laughed. "It's nice to finally meet you, Mrs. Monica Delgado."

That was a validation Monica thought she would never hear.

"Who is this man you are with?" Lola looked at Hicks with marked suspicion and a hint of dislike. "I can take you to Emma, but not him. He has to stay in town."

"No, I go with her. And I need to take Emma back with us." He flashed his credentials and some paperwork. "Understand, little lady, you are not running the show. I will be going with both of you. This is going to turn into a police matter. Emma will become the primary suspect."

"I don't care who you are, or about those pieces of paper in your pocket. You are in Merida now. We are the law here, and if we say you will stay in town, you will."

"Who's 'we'?" Hicks asked in a contemptuous manner. "The Feds were not involved in this case, and local police are shit."

Hicks's male posturing was going to destroy the only chance Monica had of seeing Emma.

Monica wanted to intervene, but she didn't want to offend Lola.

"Look around, gringo." Lola gave him a wink.

Monica and Hicks looked around the square. The town was at a standstill. Every car and bus was suddenly stopped. Every person stood frozen, statue like, staring. Some of the men had a weapon of some sort loose in their grip. They seemed to be waiting for a sign from Lola to take them down. The man who had handed him the tacos was now holding a carving knife, but he wasn't slicing onions, or anything else.

"I see. Impressive," Hicks said, taking it all in.

"You will wait here. I will bring Monica back later. Enjoy the sights and shop around. There is much to see. And as of right now, you are my guest." Lola gave him a gracious bow. "But, if you try anything, this will be your final resting place. Understand?"

189

"What are you?" Hicks's mouth spit out the words bluntly. "I mean—"

"Same as you." Lola smiled.

The words seemed to resonate with Hicks, somehow. He stared at her like she had just given him a vital clue. Perhaps Lola had information that was important to him, Monica reasoned. The way they stared at each other appeared like a silent understanding had just passed between them. Lola extended her hand to Monica. The town center came to life again as all the vendors and cars were suddenly un-paused. Monica took Lola's small hand and a feeling of instant calm coursed through her body. Her heart seemed to beat slower and the anguish she carried began melting away. She felt very safe with Lola.

They walked off arm-in-arm down the cobblestone street in the direction of the missing house, leaving Hicks speechless, holding a half-eaten taco.

33

EMMA, OPEN YOUR EYES!" ANAYA sat on the bed. "I know you're awake. We need to communicate with your ghost again."

"I was remembering my psychologist, Dr. Casey."

"The fool who thinks he can cure you?" Anaya asked.

Emma nodded. She was thinking about what Dr. Casey's assessment would be now. What rational thought or psychoanalytic theory would explain all of this? Emma kept replaying the memory of watching Valencia turn into that owl.

"Why? Why do you hate me? Is it because I'm gay?" She could feel her heart pounding. Her face flushed with embarrassment, but she needed some answers.

"Of course not, stupid—you ran from your responsibilities and left us vulnerable. We need you. I don't care who you sleep with. Enjoying women or men is natural for us. Your anxiety and illness is because you suppress great power. You are my successor. You must be strong to handle all the heartache and other problems that come with leading this coven. I imagine Daniela also struggled,"

Anaya laughed. "Everything I have done is to protect our way of life. Now, get up and pierce your tongue again. Collect the blood in this bowl. Bring the blood to me, so I can prepare the offering. You need to kill three chickens and bring them with you, too."

"Why is my aunt a fucking owl? There's no way I'm going to ignore the fact she can transform herself. Why did this happen to Daniela? What else haven't you told me?"

Emma grabbed her mother's arm and pulled her close. For the first time, Emma was not afraid. She gazed into her mother's dark brown, almost black, eyes. She used to think those eyes lacked a soul, but as she looked deeper, she could see they were filled with doubt and worry.

Anaya closed the space between them and hugged Emma tightly. "Aye, I've told you your whole life that Valencia is a nahual. We are witches, and together we form this coven—all of us, including you and Daniela. We will never grow old. We have the gift of immortality and the power of the earth. Our responsibility is to take care of others and protect our kind. Daniela is special. You knew this from her conception. She should have stayed here and trained with me, like I told you years ago. But, perhaps things happened as they were meant to. She will be the strength of this coven, the steady and constant force that keeps us all grounded."

"I was so angry with you when I got pregnant. I never wanted to be a mother. You tricked me. I didn't want Daniela to be forced into the life I walked away from. When Daniela was born, everything changed for me."

"I can't apologize. I knew we needed Daniela. I have my reasons." Anaya sighed. "My explanations will take longer than I have the time or patience for right now. Hurry up. I have a bad feeling. Summon your ghost. This is *your* power—creating and controlling familiars. You will get better at it. In the meantime, I have no memory of meeting Daniela. If she is back in time, as Beatriz claims, I don't know what could have happened to her."

The look on Anaya's face swung Emma into action. Her questions would need to wait. "Familiars?" Emma had a sudden memory of a pet bird she had as a child, a large black raven. It was always out in the yard, a constant companion. Her mom had called him a familiar also. "Like the raven, Mother? Like Fami?" Emma smiled, remembering. Growing up she had few friends. The bird helped fill the loneliness.

"Yes. You should call him too. He would love to be in your service. Fami has waited for you for a very long time. He came to me when Daniela disappeared, warning me of your distress."

"Fami lives? My god, all of this is so much." Emma walked to the window of her room and looked deep into the night, trying to wrap her mind around everything that was happening…and all that was left to do and discover. "What are you going to do with the chickens?"

Anaya didn't answer. She simply left the room quietly.

Fami, if you're out there, get your ass over here. Emma visualized the bird in her mind as Mother had instructed her to do. Anaya claimed a witch's psyche was the most powerful asset they possessed. There

193

were two threads left in her mind that she needed to pull. The first—she was a witch. The second—she would take over the Santa Muerte Coven. If she didn't embrace her own power, it would put everyone she loved at risk. Any pretense of normalcy was gone.

Emma concentrated on the shades and shadows outside her window. And there it was. A richly shimmery, black creature came from the sky, slicing the fog of night. Emma watched in awe as the raven landed on the branch of a nearby tree.

It was Fami.

MONICA AND LOLA WALKED BACK to the empty lot. There
was the large iron gate Monica and Detective Hicks had been looking for—and there was Anaya's home, tucked safely inside it.

"How? How did you hide the entire house?"

Lola rolled her eyes as she made an appreciative sound without
a formal answer.

Monica fumed as she walked behind Lola. It seemed getting any
information from this family would be impossible. As they entered
the kitchen, she felt like a live wire—frayed and dangerous to the
touch.

"Where is Emma?" Monica demanded, as she faced Anaya. The
woman looked exactly as Monica had remembered her from twenty
years ago. Ageless bitch! "Where is Emma?"

Anaya's face twisted in revolt to Monica's presence.

Monica knew Anaya hated her Puerto Rican accent. She found
it to be an abomination. Tough shit; Boricua in the house! "Well?"
Monica seethed.

"Go back home and wait for her," Anaya's hand motioned her away dismissively.

This, as intended, antagonized Monica further. "I want to see my wife. Right now!" Monica slammed her hand against the counter in fury. "You don't tell me what to do, and you don't get to decide anymore!"

Anaya raised her voice over Monica's. "Shut your mouth and get the hell out of this home, you Puerto Rican swamp rat! She is my daughter, and I am telling you that it's over!"

"I've been called worse my whole life. You think you can scare me? Even if I was the biggest whore on the planet, your daughter chose me. This is our business, and I am so tired of you meddling in our affairs. Now, where is she?" Monica was in Anaya's face feeling unconquerable confidence. "She is mine!"

Anaya wasn't budging.

Monica needed a new tactic. She took a few breaths so her heart would stop pounding, then she moved past Anaya to see what she was cooking. She needed a distraction from the yelling and wanted to give Anaya time to rethink everything. Monica wasn't backing down. On the stove were two pots, one with black beans and the other with white rice.

Monica placed the cooking spoon into the boiling beans, nabbed a few, blew on them, and tasted. "These need salt," she said with unhindered criticism. "They taste terrible—no sazon." Monica smirked triumphantly at Anaya. Gracefully, she added salt and began to fix the food.

196

Lola quickly jumped in between them and grabbed Anaya's forearm. The expression on Anaya's face was sparkling with malevolence.

Monica knew Anaya's patience was at its end. They were on the verge of fist fighting in the kitchen. Just one more condescending word from Anaya, and Monica would explode.

Lola stepped in, grabbing Anaya's forearm, stopping a near attack, speaking to Anaya in Mayan. This appeared to be of little solace.

Anaya's mouth remained twisted in an ugly expression. Monica noted it was the same grimace Emma had when looking over the credit card statements.

Anaya tried to jerk her arm away from Lola, but was unsuccessful. Lola had a lion's grip. Her voiced dropped to a hypnotic purr.

Monica didn't know what she was saying, but it seemed to be defusing the situation. Anaya looked suddenly calm.

"I've been cooking beans for three hundred years…" Anaya began, breathless like she was recovering from a workout.

"Hmm…Well I'm sure it must feel like that. Luckily, today is the first day you'll learn to do it right." Monica declared. "Go get my wife." She continued to add seasoning to the food. "Please, Anaya."

Lola and Anaya exchanged glances. Monica noted the tension was gone from their faces. She had set her limit and showed Anaya that she would back it up, even if it meant fists to face with her mother-in-law.

Anaya placed her hand gently on Lola's shoulder. "Go, Lola. Bring Emma."

Lola left the room.

Anaya tasted the beans…and, strangely, she smiled.

Monica was dismayed. They were close to having a street fight and now Anaya was suddenly calm. Was it Lola who pacified her? Surely the beans weren't that much improved…? Monica took advantage of the moment, nonetheless.

She took Anaya's hand. "No matter whatever weirdness is going on here, I want to be with Emma." *Holy shit, we're holding hands.*

†

"MONICA! WHAT ARE YOU DOING here? I asked you to wait at home." Emma froze in confusion on her way into the room. She turned to her mother. Anaya looked like she was high. Anaya swayed as she tried to turn, then steadied herself on the stove.

Emma got her mom into a chair. "Jesus, Mom. What happened to you?"

"Her? You're worried about your mother. What about me? I just flew here to find the house missing. Why are you bleeding from your mouth?"

Emma was in the middle of making her offering. She quickly grabbed a napkin from the table and pressed it over her mouth. She eyed Monica with a frown.

Monica had a confused expression on her face. Emma was sure her appearance was shocking. She was dressed oddly, in a white robe (witch garb), and had blood on her face.

Monica ran and hugged her, but Emma pushed her away. She was aware her mother was watching the whole scene and had been very clear with Emma about ending her relationship with Monica.

"You have to go back. I can't have you here. I'm not coming back until I find Daniela. I'm sorry."

Monica gaped at Emma, dazedly, as if she could not believe the words coming from her mouth. "Stop it. Just stop it! I am not going back to an empty house to wait for you. I need you. How could you just leave me like that, with no word?" Monica searched Emma's face for an answer. "What the hell are you doing here? Why aren't you helping *me* find our daughter? Why aren't we *both* working with the police? What's happening to us?"

Monica's despair did not go unnoticed by Emma, but she was close to communicating with Beatriz and needed to be at the altar. She wouldn't miss an opportunity to learn about Daniela. Monica shouldn't be here; she needed to go and leave all this behind her. Emma couldn't think of a way to make her understand.

"I have to go. I won't be coming back. I'm sorry, Monica. Do what you have to do."

"What's happened to you?" Monica grabbed Emma's shoulders and shook her. "I'm doing everything possible to find Daniela and you're here, hiding. Don't you want to find our daughter? I had to come here with a police officer. He is looking for you. Don't you care?" Monica shook Emma again, as if that would rouse her. "Look at me!"

Emma stared into her wife's beautiful brown eyes. Had Monica arrived two days ago, she would have left with her. Today, everything was different. "You're not going to understand. Even though you are Latina, this is on a whole other level of shit that I can't explain. I'm so sorry. Please, just go." *I was living a lie. I'm not even human!* A guilty voice screamed in Emma's head. She wished she could disappear so she would never have to see the horror in Monica's face if she ever discovered all she was hiding. The truth would need to wait.

"When have I ever not understood, Emma?" Monica's voice was tense.

Emma was on the verge of tears. She fought hard to remain distant and cold.

"Tell me, when? Was it when you came home pregnant? When you left us to serve in the army? When you came home with terrible PTSD? Maybe when you had the affair? Tell me when and I will leave."

Emma felt a tightness spreading from her heart to her abdomen. She wrestled with herself about what to say. Monica was right, but her mother's words remained embedded in her mind: *She will never understand our ways.*

Emma's true purpose in life was the coven, her first priority now. Pretending to be human was over. Although, Monica professed her love for Emma daily, understanding the truth and accepting it was another matter. This reality would take away the life, family, and identity Monica had relied on. It would kill her.

Even if Monica could somehow accept it all, Anaya had warned that keeping a human familiar was going to be a problem. Those types of relationships never ended well, and humans always died. Emma had to learn more about her power in order to make a decision about Monica.

"Lola, please take care of Monica for me until I finish." Emma walked out. She was unable to think of a single moment in their life together when Monica hadn't understood and forgiven her. She didn't want to fight anymore. She didn't want to cause Monica more anguish.

Lola reached for Monica's hand. Emma could see Lola's hand glow with magic. That power to comfort and calm was the only solace Emma could offer Monica. In a few moments, Monica would likely be asleep. Lulled into a false sense of serenity.

35

A DRAFT FILLED THE ROOM, awaking and alerting Daniela. She felt the beginning stages of panic creep into her body. She looked around; there was Beatriz, standing by the window in surveillance. The glass was frosted over and the room felt like a freezer. Beatriz had talked to her about the different levels of cold she could emanate. This was intense. This meant something bad was about to happen.

"Get up. We have company." Beatriz remained vigilant.

Daniela put on a shirt and tucked it into her pants. She looked out the window, seeing nothing but a blanket of mist that engulfed the dirt road below.

"I don't see anyone. Who's there?" Daniela's lips tightened in apprehension when she saw the mask of concern on Beatriz's face.

"La negra. She is hiding in the mist." Beatriz turned and looked at Daniela. "She came for you. She will try to hurt you. Do you want me to take over?"

Daniela sensed the danger in the situation, looked around the room, grabbed the gun on the dresser, loaded it. "No, I can handle it." This time she didn't feel frozen in confusion.

She thought about who "the negra" could be—perhaps another friend of Lain's? She stood by the window next to Beatriz. The mist cleared just enough to get a decent glimpse. It was a black woman, alright. Seeing Sabine crouched by a tree was a delight Daniela was not prepared for. She yelped in joy, opened the window. "Sabine! Sabine! It's me, Daniela!" She waved vigorously down to her aunt.

Beatriz kept insisting she close the window.

Daniela ignored her. "I'm coming down! Wait for me!" Daniela darted out the door, leaving Beatriz far behind....

Once outside, Daniela looked frantically for Sabine. She felt overwhelming waves of relief to finally have someone she loved here to help. *How was Sabine here?* She looked exactly the same as she did in 2030. Had her mother and grandmother sent Sabine to find her? Daniela looked longingly toward the tree where she had spotted Sabine, but she was gone.

Is this a dream? She suddenly wondered about that, but continued her search.

Beatriz called out, "Daniela, prepare your gun. She's coming around again."

Daniela turned to answer when she felt cold steel pressed tightly against her neck—a knife. It was so hard against her skin she couldn't swallow. Warm blood began trickling down her throat.

"Who are you?" Sabine's voice was like acid; she pressed harder, drastically reducing Daniela's air supply.

"It's... me, Tia...Daniela," she managed to choke out.

Sabine was holding her arm so tightly Daniela felt it was on the verge of breaking.

"I'm Anaya's granddaughter. Don't you remember me?"

"Anaya doesn't have children, you liar. Now, you are going to tell me exactly what you're doing here." Sabine released her arm and pushed her to the ground. Daniela landed on her face,

her tears of joy souring as they mixed with the dirt.

"You have ten seconds." Sabine slid the knife she had pressed against Daniela's neck into a scabbard strapped across her chest.

Daniela exhaled a small breath of relief.

Then Sabine pulled out a machete that was strapped to her leg. "This will be a swift kill. You seem to have little experience, and the spirit is unable take possession."

In spite of the big knife, Daniela scrambled to her feet and ran to Sabine, placing her arms around her in a tight embrace. "Please, Tia. You don't know me yet. I wasn't born until 2010. My mom is Emma, and Anaya is my grandmother. Look at my face, for God's sake!"

Daniela felt a warm sensation spreading out on the left side of her stomach. When she looked down there was a pool of blood. Sabine had stabbed her, and the machete was lodged deep inside. Daniela stared down in disbelief.

Something in Sabine's expression suddenly changed when she reached for the amethyst charm around Daniela's neck.

"How did you get this?" she shook Daniela. "Answer me!"

Daniela dropped down, her knees giving out beneath her. She grasped the machete, unsure if she should pull it out. The pain was rapidly becoming unbearable.

"Jesus, you do look just like Anaya. Oh my god! It's true!" Sabine grabbed Daniela's face and peered into her eyes. "Hold on, I can fix you. Don't move."

"You stabbed me. What the fuck?" Daniela looked at the embedded machete again, as she slowly slid into shock. She reached for Sabine's hand. It was ice cold.

Sabine's teeth chattered as she talked to Daniela. "I won't hurt you. Ask your ghost to relax, please. I have to remove my knife and heal the wound and I can't do it if my hands are like ice!"

"Relax, Beatriz. Relax...." Daniela sounded drunk with delirium.

Sabine clenched her fist, trying to warm her hands. Once relieved of the intense cold, she went to work. She dislodged the machete in a swift movement.

Her eyes were closed. She was quietly chanting.

"Do you stab a lot of people?" Daniela studied Sabine's familiar face. "You seemed to know what you were doing. And you're really strong too, Sabine. I didn't know that about you."

"Why aren't you regenerating?" Sabine sounded exasperated.

Daniela shrugged and looked down at the open wound. "I need stitches. You expect the wound to magically close or something?"

"Yes. The wound should magically close. You're a witch! We regenerate from injury," Sabine mocked. "Stop smiling at me like that! You look like you found a puppy, for God's sake." Sabine reached over and ripped some fabric off Daniela's clothes. "How old are you? Why aren't you healing?"

Daniela laughed, "I think I'm going into shock. I'm twenty. Seriously, you have to sew it or something, before I bleed out."

Sabine laughed, "Only me. I swear, this would only happen to me. I couldn't mess up any more if I tried. Anaya is right. I'm a walking disappointment."

"I've never seen you so frazzled, Sabine. Were you looking for me and just didn't recognize me? How did you come back in time?"

"Back in time? It's 1923. I was looking for a rogue witch who almost killed Lain and is using the coven name for self-gain. What the hell are you talking about?" Sabine continued to tend to the wound.

The bleeding was slowing down. Daniela had a sensation of warmth in her body.

"There you go. You're starting to regenerate. Congratulations: you are an immortal, kid."

Daniela chuckled.

They stared at one another, oddly jubilant. Daniela wanted to embrace her again, but didn't have all her strength back yet.

"You do this a lot, you know," Daniela said.

"What's that?" Sabine asked.

"Laugh. In the future, I mean. We're happy. We're not a bunch of angry, stabbing witches." Daniela gazed at Sabine, searching for subtle differences. "If you're not from my time, then why do you look the same?"

"I'm one hundred years old now. I stopped aging at thirty-five. It could be that I end up living another hundred years looking the same." Tears welled in her eyes. She cried as she inspected Daniela's wound. "Happy. Alive. You use those words so easily. Surely you must mean someone else?"

"No, you're alive...and happy in 2030. I love you so much, Tia. I'm just so lucky you're here." Daniela gently touched Sabine's face, wiping away the tears. "How did you find me? You really think I'm a witch, too?"

"Gee, kid. If you don't know anything about yourself, that's very troubling." Sabine held her hand over the wound as white light emanated from it.

"We are a coven of witches, the Santa Muerte Coven. We are immortal, and your grandmother is the head bitch." Sabine helped Daniela up. "Yes, we all have magical powers, and it seems yours is the ability to open time portals. Somehow your magic was activated, and here you are." Sabine shrugged. "That's the simplest explanation that I can think of."

"Is this what they mean when the people of this time use the word 'speakeasies'?" Daniela laughed again. "You just drop a bomb-shell and proceed as usual—*speaking real easy* about me being a time-traveling immortal witch."

Sabine laughed a little. "No, a speakeasy is…look, never mind."

Daniela dropped her head, back to feeling the weight of the world on her shoulders. She felt her left side; her shirt was still soaked with blood but the wound was closed, the pain gone. "Okay, so, how do I use my powers? How can I get back home, Tia? Can you show me?"

"Yes, well, we'll find a way to understand it once we're back at the coven." Sabine assured her. "What happened, anyway? How did you first use your power? And why are you dressed like a man?"

Daniela wanted to blurt everything out, but where to even begin….

"Sit. This may take a bit." She waved Beatriz over to join them. "The danger's over. Come on…."

Daniela started with her suicide attempt and all that had tran-spired since her arrival. Sabine sat next to her, listening intently. Daniela confessed every thought releasing it all hoping Sabine would absolve her of her sins, somehow. They sat in silence after the story for some time, thinking it all over.

Something finally occurred to Daniela. "Hey, how come you didn't remember us meeting in the future and warn me about all this?"

"I didn't know. I've heard theories about time travel. Maybe time flows concurrently, or maybe you were always meant to travel back to this time."

"Hey, maybe it's like that movie, *Back to the Future*." Daniela smiled, recalling that favorite movie franchise from her childhood. Then her heart sank. "But he ends up causing changes in the past that create new timelines in the future. That could be really bad. What about Lain? Is he a time traveler too? "

"Well, I don't know about any movie. Anaya would know best. She's the oldest witch on Earth. There is nothing she hasn't encountered. Lain is our enemy. He's not a time traveler, but I imagine he wishes he could be. He can use the Spirit Realm to travel, but not through time. He has the ability to show up out of nowhere, like a spirit. So we must always be careful." Sabine glanced around.

"Why is he an enemy?" Daniela checked behind her, just in case he was lurking on the other side of the tree.

"He's a bloodletter. His kind gets off on hurting people and creating devastation wherever they go. Trust me—he never helps anyone without it serving his own interests. When your grandmother gets her hands on him...it's gonna be real bad."

Daniela smiled at the thought of her grandmother kicking ass. "You know, considering all the bad choices I've made, this haircut was weirdly genius." Her perspective was changing. "Being able to pass as a boy probably saved my life."

"Yeah, well, next time go with a bob." Sabine jabbed at her playfully. "We have to get back to the tree. Anaya wouldn't want me to return without some kind of evidence of your claim. I must bring her some soil and bark from the tree. Then she can give us answers and decide what to do with you. What did you call it, the Devil's Oak? Maybe it is a portal or wormhole. You must have conjured enough negative energy to open it. Speak to your spirit. Find out more about what she knows of the future. She is our link. If time is running concurrently, then she can speak to your mother, who can help us."

36

BEATRIZ FINALLY ARRIVED AT THE coven; she had felt
Emma's call all night—like an invisible rope tied to her waist pulling
her back to Merida and 2030. Beatriz was yanked directly into the
prayer room housing a stone altar filled with candles and incense.
Pictures of various saints and offerings of hair, umbilical cords, and
dried skin hung near the altar. A long oak table was in the center of
the room filled with candles and a display of traditional foods for
her choosing. Beatriz was starved. Spirits needed only to smell the
food and they could take the flavor from it and have the sense of
being full. She saw Emma there, praying with all her might—eyes
squeezed shut, lips moving in double-time, reciting the same prayer
over and over—but hunger took precedence. Beatriz used both
hands to bring food near her mouth. She inhaled deeply and
watched the chicken become rancid and shriveled, a dried-out husk.
She placed it back on the plate. Emma would want answers. How
could she tell Emma that every time she turned, Daniela stepped
into a bigger pile of shit? The girl was heedless, a disaster, and a

mediocre witch at best. The spells and chants Beatriz tried to teach her had yet to work. Daniela refused to believe what she was capable of, instead listening to the insecurity in her own mind.

Beatriz felt better now, stronger, mostly satisfied. She reached for dessert—a bowl filled with blood. She would need every last drop, and could consume the blood unlike the food. She was delighted by the amount, even though it was the least Emma could do for the predicament she had placed her in. The blood was warm and nourishing. Beatriz used her finger—like a kid would with frosting in a bowl—to get the last bits into her mouth. She watched cautiously as Emma continued to pray in supplication, tears now streaming down her cheeks.

Ugh, these girls love to cry.

Beatriz allowed the bowl to drop, alerting Emma of her presence.

"Please, tell me, Beatriz—what's going on with Daniela? Is she all right?" Emma jumped right into pleading.

"Call the elder witch. I will need more spells," Beatriz replied, casually. She reached over and made herself another taco. "These beans are really good, by the way." She smiled at Emma. Beatriz could sense Emma's anxiety but she did not have time for questions. "Quickly—we don't have much time. I must return to Daniela. Call the elder."

Emma opened her eyes and walked to the door, calling urgently for her mother.

Anaya appeared instantly. Anaya's impatience seemed to rival Beatriz's. Nonetheless, she sat near the altar and closed her eyes ceremoniously.

Beatriz faced Anaya when she spoke.

Emma relayed the message. "Daniela remains in danger. She is in Mexico, with la negra, but they are going back to the tree. Sabine wants to examine the portal herself."

"La negra? Go and fetch Sabine, Emma. Now!" Anaya demanded. "She will clarify for us."

Emma rose and ran out.

"Listen to me, Beatriz," Anaya seethed, "I am no fool. You are getting stronger with each offering. I want Daniela here. Now! Your time is running out. I will do far worse than burn your cross. Your family will pay for your ineptitude if one hair on the head of my granddaughter is harmed. We both understand each other, don't we?"

Beatriz nodded. She understood Anaya had the power to devastate generations-worth of her family. Keeping the girl safe was a small price to pay for their safety and she was beginning to imagine the rewards that were possible for her dutiful service.

Emma was breathless upon her return. "She's gone. Sabine is gone." Emma held a box in her hands. "She went to find Valencia. This package arrived today. It's from someone named Lain." She tore open the parcel. Inside were Valencia's long, magnificent owl feathers with a note: *Thanks.*

"Thanks. That's all it says. Who's Lain? Why are Valencia's feathers in here?" Emma demanded of her mother.

Anaya exhaled a deep sighed. "Come, Emma, let me teach you both some more spells. Your familiar must get back quickly." Anaya's face darkened. Fatigue settled in the lines of her forehead. She seemed lost in deep thought and calculations.

"I must know what she really is. And tell me what her power is." Beatriz had sensed Daniela was more than just a witch from the start. The elder witch had run out of time for keeping the secret.

Emma translated and added, "Mom, what does she mean? More than just a witch?"

"She seems to have some of her father in her. That much is clear."

"Her father? You said he would never be an issue!"

"She is more witch than anything else, so he doesn't matter." Anaya waved dismissively. "Her power is time travel and manipulating portals, but she does not yet know how to control them. You must guide her, Beatriz. Getting Daniela home is the only concern; we cannot get sidetracked. Come, let me give you these spells and explain how to use the Devil's Oak portal. Tell Sabine to bring her directly to me. I will not need proof about the tree."

Anaya walked over to the altar and removed a dusty book from a shelf close by. She hastily flipped through some pages, then started chanting in Mayan.

Beatriz paid careful attention. They were simple rhymes she could easily teach Daniela. She had to hurry; this much time away could mean all kinds of trouble.

37

"WHY ARE WE GOING BACK to New Jersey? Why don't we just go see my grandmother now?" Daniela was bewildered. The journey to Mexico had taken several days. She didn't want to miss an opportunity for her grandmother to help her.

"We're going to use a travel portal, Daniela. It will take mere minutes to reach New Jersey, and we can get back here just as quickly. We use portals similar, I imagine, to what you used to travel to 1923—but yours was a time portal."

Sabine walked briskly, deeper into the Yucatan jungle. The lights from the town center faded behind them as Daniela followed.

She struggled to comprehend what Sabine claimed. "If people are traveling this way, how come no one else knows about it?" Daniela stumbled in the darkness while Sabine marched steady onward.

"Immortals use travel portals to reach different destinations all over earth, as well as the Realms. Not humans. They do not know of our existence. I will teach you more about that some other time."

"Yes, Lain mentioned Realms. What the hell are those?" This was baptism by fire. Everything had changed in a span of three weeks, and then again, in the span of three minutes.

Sabine used her machete to clear a path and kept moving forward. "Portals are found in many different places. You see there?" Sabine pointed to a Ceiba tree, deeper yet into the jungle. "Do you see the way the moonlight hits the branches? It creates that glow? That is a travel portal. They are like tiny geomagnetic storms."

"I don't see it. All moonlight glows."

Daniela was squinting in the direction in which Sabine had pointed, but there was nothing there.

"You'll see it better when we arrive." Sabine swung an arm back, yanked Daniela forward. "Any word from your spirit?"

"No, nothing. She said she would be back, though, so she will be." Daniela looked around. She neither saw nor felt Beatriz anywhere. Nothing but mugginess in this dark jungle.

"It makes me uneasy, the relationship you have with that spirit. The way in which you are able to talk to Beatriz and see her is unusual."

"Wait, I see it!" Daniela exclaimed. Next to the tree were faint colors similar to the Northern Lights in Alaska—pale pink and green in scattered patches. Obvious once she saw them. "There. There's the faint outline of the portal against the tree. I see it."

Sabine crouched down in the brush, pulling Daniela with her. "Easy. We're not the only ones who use portals, or see them."

They crawled from that point on. After a few moments, they emerged and stood in front of the Ceiba tree; its massive roots spread across the jungle floor like they were the earth's fingers.

"When we enter the travel portal, just hold my hand and close your eyes. You might feel some motion sickness the first time. Well, the second time...." Sabine extended her hand.

Daniela took it, grasping on for dear life.

"Picture where we are going in your mind."

Daniela pictured her house in her mind.

"Got it?"

"Yes, I got it."

"Okay, close your eyes and hold onto me."

Daniela's eyes were clamped shut. Her bottom lip trembled with anxiety.

As Sabine pulled her forward, Daniela felt her stomach drop, as if she were on a steep, spiraling roller coaster. She screamed, tightening her vice-grip on Sabine's hand as the sensation continued. Daniela could feel her hair whipping against her face. A strong force hit her like a fifty-pound weight, slamming against her chest and knocking the wind out of her. Oddly, she could still breathe, and it didn't feel like any ribs were broken. She felt lightheaded and sick to her stomach. She was too fearful to open her eyes. Then everything stopped—the weight left her chest, the wind stilled, the queasiness vanished. She fell to her knees onto what seemed to be wet grass. She could smell a forest, and water. Daniela opened her eyes. She became dizzy and disoriented all over again.

"It's okay. We're here. I think...." Sabine released her hand from Daniela's. "Swampland?" she asked.

Daniela looked around in disbelief. She stood up slowly, recognizing the lake. Her ears were ringing. "I was thinking about home. We're about three miles from the tree." Daniela was on the move. She knew the route well, having jogged it a thousand times. She felt déjà vu as her walk turned into a jog and she ran toward her absolution again.

Sabine was close behind.

"There it is!" Daniela exclaimed in excitement.

"Wait, Daniela. We're not alone," Sabine warned.

Daniela only half heard her. The ringing in her ears had lessened, but she was so excited to be back, she steamed ahead. What if she could open the portal again and just go home? Her determination to reach the tree superseded her impatience and judgment.

And then she saw them: Men dressed in white robes and hoods.

Daniela shivered as they approached the tree. She froze in fear. The stories she had read about the KKK had turned her stomach, but that was nothing compared to the feeling she had now.

Sabine pulled Daniela close.

"Ward yourself!" She commanded. Sabine began chanting in Spanish.

Daniela tried to repeat what she was saying.

Distracted, neither one saw a man come from behind. And then it was too late. He had Daniela in a chokehold, and managed to grab Sabine by the hair.

More men came at them. Sabine fought back, flipping one of the men over her shoulder and stabbing another one behind her, ready to fight off more.

Dozens of white robed men ran to the aid of their clan members. Sabine and Daniela were outnumbered in no time.

The first attacker released Daniela. She screamed just as a chain lassoed her.

"Treat 'em rough, boys!" the hooded man called out. "Roger, is this your boy?" The man on the end of the chain pulled, dragging Daniela through the grass by her neck. Sabine lunged at Daniela. She dug her fingers underneath the chain in an attempt to loosen it. She, too, was now being dragged. Another man approached, sliced Sabine's right hand off just below the wrist. Sabine balled up, writhing in pain. Daniela could feel Sabine's hand still stuck in the chain around her neck. More men surrounded Sabine tightening a chain around her body and dragging her.

"We need help, here! This one's strong!" The man yelled.

Despite being tied, Sabine fought them hard, with the bravery of a lioness protecting her pride. Daniela struggled for air as the chain continued to compress her throat.

Roger knelt down next to her. He punched Daniela in the stomach, and pulled her up by her hair until she was on her knees. "I'm only gonna ask you once. If you lie to me, I'll let the mob have you." He spit chewing tobacco on Daniela's face and wiped the remaining saliva from his mouth on her body. "Where is Daphne?" He swung

Daniela around, so she could see the mob of men waiting by a burning cross. He whispered in her ear, "Now, that mob is gonna burn
you alive. But before they do, they'll want to hurt you, real bad."

The men began chanting when they saw Roger's prize.

Daniela's body shook in his arms, ravaged with despair. "I don't
know. I'm so sorry. We lost each other in New York."

Roger spit on her again, this time the large, brown, saliva-soaked
bundle he was holding in his bottom lip. "String 'em up!" he ordered.

The sound of the cheers resembled a football stadium. The men
were starving for blood and violence. Daniela could see Sabine still
fighting.

"The more you struggle, the worse it will be for the boy." Roger
continued to callously beat Daniela while he threatened Sabine.

There were men lying on the ground near Sabine, dead; their
white robes blood-soaked. Sabine stopped fighting. Daniela was
badly injured. She coughed up blood.

A man wearing a military uniform walked over and placed his
hand on Roger's shoulder. He let go of Daniela. They studied Sabine
in an odious manner. Daniela took this opportunity to curl herself
into a ball. Her body was so hot, trying to regenerate from the
wounds.

"I told you—they are not like us." In his hand, the military man
held some kind of meter and was showing Roger and the other men.
"We have to find them and kill them all. Imagine monsters like this

221

everywhere, killing. This bitch just murdered five of my men." He leaned down and placed the meter near Daniela's body.

A loud beeping sounded from the black object in the man's hand. "It's a radiation meter. These animals give off higher levels of it." The military man placed the meter next to Roger and there was a small clicking. Then he moved it back to Daniela. The high-pitched beep went off and held steady again. It was a violent alarm, really off-putting. Roger and the other men came in closer to read the meter.

The piercing sound of the meter rang in Daniela's ears long after the man had moved it away. It reminded her of when a person flat-lines. Was she about to die? Her mind wandered, almost hoping so. She closed her eyes, hoping she'd pass out, but awoke to the sound of more violence.

The military man kicked Sabine in the stomach, then in the face.

Another man in uniform was going through Daniela's bag. He grabbed her phone and handed it to the man who was kicking Sabine.

That man nodded approvingly, and then signaled to his men that it was time to leave. "Can I trust you, Roger, to take care of these two? My boss needs this." He looked carefully at Daniela's phone. "Getting it to him now is the mission."

Roger answered by dragging Daniela toward the tree. She struggled. He kicked her until she was still and her body went limp.

Cheers continued and the demand to "string 'em up" was again chanted. The crowd moved in closer.

Two men came over and tied Sabine and Daniela with rope around their necks. They were hoisted up high to allow everyone a first-class seat to the lynching. Before their necks snapped, they were dropped back down and whipped by men from behind. Daniela felt the rope strain against her neck again as she was lifted. She saw Roger and another man dump pieces of wood underneath the tree and start a fire.

It was hard to see, strung up like that. She could hear Sabine scream. She caught a glimpse of a group of men pulling on the chain to keep Sabine in the fire. Unable to scream herself, she stopped fighting, hoping to just die. Her body was dropped suddenly into the fire, her skin and hair burning. Then, once again, she was hoisted up to slowly choke some more.

A powerful gust of cold wind shocked her senses. She opened her eyes. The fire was out. Roger and the men stopped chanting. They dropped the women. Daniela could feel that the logs of wood underneath her body had iced over.

She passed out, no longer able to bear the horror.

TAKING POSSESSION OF DANIELA'S BODY was a cinch this time around. With Emma's fresh blood in her system, Beatriz felt stronger than ever. She stood and ripped the chain from around Daniela's neck like a little girl's charm necklace.

"Basta!" Beatriz cackled. With that, men near the fire pit shot fifty feet into the air and fell to the ground, moaning. Other men immediately ran to their aid. Sabine was still dangling awkwardly from the noose. Beatriz pulled her down, and waited for the men to attack. The ones who reached her first stopped and made a sign of the cross when they caught a good look.

One screamed, "It's the devil! It's Satan himself!"

Beatriz smiled at the man shaking violently under his white sheet. She imagined the sight of Daniela would instill fear in anyone. She gave them a shrill shriek and sent most of them scurrying. The ones who remained had no chance against her. She quickly dispatched them with Sabine's machete. More men in the distance ran to assist. At this point, Beatriz was getting bored and wanted to leave.

"Vamos, negra!" Beatriz smacked Sabine's cheek to stir her.

Sabine roused, clutched the stump where her hand once resided, and clung to Beatriz.

Beatriz could feel the energy from the Devil's Oak. Streaming red lights emanated from it as its portal opened. It was now or never. Beatriz flung Sabine over her shoulder and grabbed the chain attached to the tree to pull them in. Once inside the time portal, they disappeared from the men, entering what looked to be an endless black tunnel.

Beatriz felt a stinging sensation. Aching overtook Daniela's body. Sabine started screaming in agony. Travel through this portal was particularly painful. Beatriz knew that she had to move quickly despite the ache deep in her bones. She turned her body against the energy that pushed them forward; her neck snapped back from its power, but she wasn't knocked down. Anaya had instructed her to move against the pull of the portal to move toward the future; moving with the pull of portal would send them back further in time. Beatriz could feel Daniela's bones cracking from the pressure. Time was rushing past them in a whirl of colors. The force against her chest was immense. She just had to reach the end of the tunnel to get Daniela back to her time. Daniela's body was strong enough to take the pressure and the pain. It had to be. Beatriz willed her body forward repeating over and over that she was strong enough. She was strong enough. She was enough....

38

"CALLEN—LOOK AT THIS MESSAGE and tell me who sent it." Lain studied his phone curiously. The text from Daniela read: *Test.*

Callen was still seated comfortably on the bed, despite the order.

Having tracked Daniela to a shitty boarding house in Mexico and finding an empty room was disappointment enough for Lain. But this *subordinate* avoiding questions and ignoring orders was—"Now! Callen, you fucking dog!" He threw the phone.

Callen caught it, held it tight in his grip. He closed his eyes and took a deep breath. "Men. It's not the girl."

"Do you sense anything else?"

"Military." Callen tossed the phone back to Lain. "Bad vibes."

"Wonderful. That stupid bitch got herself caught."

This was a real problem for the witches. If the technology fell into the wrong hands, this could mean devastation for all of them. The Realms would never let them back, or bother to help them.

"Let's go," Lain said. "Track where this text came from and get me to Daniela."

Lain hated that every time he uttered Daniela's name, he had to fight the urge to smile. He erased the thought, hoping Callen didn't sense it.

"Looks like we finally have something in common, Lain."

"Grab your shit, and let's go." Lain realized he needed to be better at shielding his thoughts. He was going to be with Callen for a while and had too many secrets to protect. *How did she defeat Sabine? Could Daniela be dead? Why do I fuckin' care?*

"We just have to get the phone, you asshole. Quit dwelling on your schoolboy crush—"

Lain flipped, grabbed Callen by the collar of his shirt, and slammed him against the wall with enough force to knock him out (had he been human). He kept his elbow on Callen's windpipe, controlling each gasp. Lain was eye to eye with the dog, letting every evil thought of what he would do flow unfiltered into Callen's mind.

Callen slowly nodded in silent understanding.

"Stay out of my head." Lain struggled to keep his voice level and his emotions under control. He released another image of Callen dying by torture. Lain took his time in releasing the pressure on Callen's throat. Lain enjoyed watching him writhe. Seeing the veins in his neck engorged with blood while his body fought instinctively—was thrilling. It made Lain feel omnipotent. Callen's lips were blue by now, but not blue enough. Lain pressed harder, just one more time. Callen began to pass out.

"Let's go." Lain reluctantly released him. He remembered Callen had access to information about Daniela. He still needed him. Not as much as he wanted Daniela, though.

39

DANIELA AWOKE. SHE WAS COUGHING, like she was choking again. Then seized with revulsion at the smell of burnt hair and skin. Her body hurt. Like the last time she had time traveled, she felt like she had been in a car accident. Her neck was tender, and she could hear the sound of her bones moving as she turned her head. Everything around her was eerily silent; the mob was gone.

"Sabine!"

"I couldn't hold you both for long. I had to leave her at the closest opening inside the portal. She will be safe. We can return for her later." Beatriz was by Daniela's side. "The pain will pass quickly. Get up. You're home."

"Home?"

"Is this not your time?"

Daniela was lying next to the big oak with the brilliant red leaves. Even at night they defiantly shimmered. Daniela pulled herself up and looked around. Nearby, she could see the dog park. She smiled.

"I'm home. I can see my neighborhood." The familiar sounds were all around once she took notice. It gave Daniela the energy to stand and start limping home.

"How did you do it? I mean, how are we here?" Everything felt like a dream, much like the fogginess upon waking up after a long surgery. Her mind felt numb, but the compulsion to keep walking was primal. She picked up the pace. Even if this was a dream, she wanted to at least see her house one last time.

"I will show you, next time." Beatriz laughed a little. "Easy—you are practically running. You heal quickly now."

"There it is! Oh my god." Daniela pointed to her house, elated. "What time is it? All the lights are out they must be in bed."

"Your mother is in Mexico, remember?"

The door opened once the facial recognition lens scanned her and allowed her access. The familiar smell of home surrounded her like a warm blanket.

"Welcome home, Daniela." The robotic annunciation of her name was like heaven. She started to cry.

"Mom! Mom!" She screamed, running toward the bedrooms upstairs. Her mom Monica had to be home.

"Mom!" Daniela sobbed by the stairs, unable to remove herself from the railing. "Mom, I'm back. I'm sorry! I'm so sorry."

"There is no one here, niña. This house is empty." Beatriz called to her from the kitchen. "Mira." She held up a printed itinerary to Mexico. "Your other mother left too."

Daniela wiped her eyes with the back of her hand and went into the kitchen. The motion sensor lights efficiently illuminated the space.

"What day is it, Otaku?" Daniela called out.

The computer-generated voice answered. "Today is November 30, 2030, Daniela. The time is 3:33 a.m. Eastern Standard Time. Monica and Emma are in Merida, Mexico. The return itinerary has not been uploaded at this time."

Beatriz looked around amazed, trying to locate the voice. On the counter, a small white machine moved forward.

"Que es?"

"She's like a robot. I call her Otaku, though." Daniela answered casually. She began to rummage around for some food.

The robot moved across the large center island, scanning the refrigerator. "The milk has expired. Do not drink. You have one voicemail. Shall I play it?" The robot continued to scan the room.

"Who's it from?"

"Caller is...Lain."

Daniela dropped the expired milk on the floor. "Yes, play it." She dropped down with a towel to wipe up the mess. Her hands trembled from the sudden chill; Beatriz was on high alert.

"Upstairs." Lain's voice played calmly.

"The message is complete. Shall I connect you to the—"

"No, not now. Power down. Thank you, Otaku." Daniela scanned her surroundings, checking for other threats.

231

Beatriz nodded and looked at the knives on the counter, encouraging Daniela to take one.

Daniela slid one out carefully and began to make her way up the steps. Her heart started pounding in her chest.

"Do you want me to take over?" Beatriz was at her side, ready. Daniela fought the urge to let her. She had to do this.

"No, but you can take the lead."

Gently, Daniela opened her bedroom door. Beatriz glided in.

"Lain," Daniela could see her breath as she called for him. It was like walking into a subzero meat locker. To freeze the room like this, Beatriz had to be extremely worried. Lain was here, somewhere. Daniela took a step back, deciding suddenly not to go further.

"Peek-a-boo."

Startled, Daniela dropped the knife.

"Relax. You would have been dead from the moment you touched the front door if I had wanted." Lain appeared out of nowhere, gave her the queerest look, then flashed her his brilliant smile. He looked the same, except he was dressed in modern clothes that looked really expensive. *Didn't lose the flair for fashion.*

"What do you want? Why are you here?"

"What I've always wanted, Daniela." He seized her arms, pulled her to his chest, and kissed her forcefully.

Caught off-guard, she collapsed into the kiss momentarily, then common sense shot into her like a bullet from a gun, and she shoved him back hard.

"Very well. Tit for tat."

"What the hell does that mean?" Daniela could feel her lips tingling, her cheeks flushing. She touched her mouth.

"You want another one?" Lain smiled, deviously.

"No." Daniela took another step back. More distance was best. "Where is Daphne?"

Lain had a puzzled look on his face, like he was trying to recall a remote memory. "You are quite the troublemaker, Daniela. But looking at you makes it all worth it." Lain's eyes lingered all over her body, making her feel totally exposed, like someone had just snatched her bath towel. His eyes darted to Beatriz. He gave her a menacing look that transformed his face from handsome prince into lethal creature. He spoke in a language Daniela didn't understand, but she knew what he was saying was full of malice.

"Stop it!" Daniela positioned herself between Lain and Beatriz. "I won't let you hurt her."

"She and I have a score to settle; another time, perhaps." Lain reached into his pocket. Then he took Daniela's hand in his, turned it over, placed her phone into it. "A gift for you, my love."

"How did you get this? Those racist mother—"

"Easy now." Lain caressed her arm. "You owe me." His voice took an ominous tone.

Daniela knew those words were never good. She didn't dare move. She, in fact, kept her hand in his and inched closer. She told herself, she, too, had tactics. But the longer she maintained eye contact, the harder it was to focus. "Okay, Lain, answer me, then. How? Why are you really here? How did you know I would be here?"

Lain lingered, allowing Daniela to take him in, to breathe him in—then vanished.

"Lain. Lain!" Daniela spun around. "Where the fuck did he go?"

"He's gone. Good riddance. Remember, he is a bloodletter. He can travel in the Spirit Realm. This is why I did not sense him when we arrived." Beatriz sat on the bed. "Who knows how long he's been here. He's trouble. Be careful, Daniela."

"Oh god, Beatriz. Can you please start making sense? I need to get to Sabine, Daphne, my moms. I need to go to Mexico. I don't know what all this means." Daniela put her phone back in what was left of her pocket, then walked into her private bathroom and started the shower. One glimpse of herself in the mirror made it clear why Lain had looked at her so strangely. She had seen zombies on TV look better than she did now. The steam filled the bathroom as Daniela stripped the burnt fabric off her body. She got her best ideas in the shower.

"Beatriz!" Daniela called from the bathroom.

Beatriz floated into the room.

"We're going back to the portal."

"Esta bien." Beatriz agreed. Then she explained how the portal worked and what she would need to do.

Daniela got out of the shower, wiped the steam from the mirror, and connected her phone to it. Pictures of Daphne appeared, making the knot in her throat unbearable. She called her mom Emma, not knowing what time it was in Mexico.

"Bueno."

"Abuela?"

"Mm...Daniela. Que paso, chiquita? Nos tienes preucupadas."

"I'm sorry, Grandma. I didn't mean to worry everyone. I made some terrible mistakes, but I'm home now. I'm okay, I'm at the house."

"Oh thank God." Emma appeared on the screen next to Anaya. "I'm sorry. I didn't know about all of this magic and stuff. You must have been going out of your mind. I should have—"

"No, Mom, it's not your fault. I was too scared to tell you so many things." Daniela wiped away tears.

"Me too. I was too." A moment of silence passed between them. In true Emma style, she tried to lighten the mood. "Hey, did you get my gift?"

"Yeah. Thank you. Beatriz has been awesome. How in the world were you able to send her?"

"You're not the only one discovering new things about yourself."

"Tell me, where is Sabine?" Anaya interrupted.

Daniela scratched her head nervously. How to explain? "She's in the portal. Beatriz left her in the nearest opening. I have to go back to get her. I'm okay. I feel better. Stronger."

"You are reborn into the witch you are meant to be. There is much to do. First, find Sabine. She is in danger. We need her back. It's many years since she was lost."

"I'm leaving. I'll get her." Daniela's stomach sank; she needed to help Daphne, but Sabine's situation was as dangerous. The tone of her grandmother's voice made the hair on her arms stand on end.

"Mmm...Lain," Anaya mused. "Remember, dos agujas no se pican. Trust no one. You have much to do and you never disappoint me, mi niña. Seven years ago, you came to see me—in time, you will begin to remember. Use your spells. Believe in your magic. Know we are always connected."

Daniela felt a weight on her shoulders. Insecurity swirled in her mind.

"We are all scared sometimes, but we must still act. We believe in you and will continue our link with Beatriz. May God bless you and keep you safe. Te amo." Anaya looked over at Emma.

"Good Luck, Daniela. We'll be here in Mexico, waiting for your return."

"Yeah. I'll be home soon. I love you too." She blew them a kiss before disconnecting the call.

Daniela looked at herself in the mirror. She strained to recall any details about her last trip to Mexico. There was nothing. She had a memory of coming home, but everything else was unclear. Daniela studied herself, noticing she appeared older somehow, even though that was impossible. She felt physically stronger than ever. Emotionally, she began to feel something she could only categorize as confidence. The angst and frustration within her was gone. The ongoing sensation of not feeling right in her body was fast becoming a distant memory.

She ran her fingers through her hair. The pixie—a stunt to make her appear foreign to her moms looked right now. It looked good. It added edge. Daniela opened the bottom drawer of her vanity, grabbed her Wahl razor, and flipped it on. It vibrated subtly in her hand. She pressed it against her head and started carving a symbol into her scalp. As strange as it was, her newfound purpose in life— a powerful witch destined to serve her coven—made sense. It suddenly became the most obvious answer to all her disconnected feelings from the past. She was gonna be one badass witch—that's what she told herself. But why...why hadn't she known sooner? Daniela adorned the other side with another symbol, and trimmed the top of her hair. Fitting in was no longer a concern.

Fuckin' Lain. She touched her mouth. Her Achilles' heel was shitty relationships. Her grandma was right: trust no one. Maybe not even herself. Daniela moved to the bedroom and packed a duffle bag with supplies, while her phone synced with all the updates and history of the 1920s.

This time she would be prepared.

END of BOOK ONE

ACKNOWLEDGEMENTS

It is with gratitude and humility that I would like to thank my family for their unwavering support of this book. My wonderful husband, Michael: Thank you for always believing in me and encouraging me to write. My beautiful daughters, Juliana and Olivia: you inspire me everyday, I love you. My brother, Angelo, who understood this book from the first paragraph: thank you for cheering me on. Thank you, Mom, for always sharing your strange stories and scaring me to death as a child. Thank you for living your life fearlessly and never settling. To my grandmothers—you've inspired me from heaven. To my father, who might not understand it all, thanks for loving me, regardless.

I would love to acknowledge Lisa Cerasoli who edited the shit out of this book and helped me to deliver the story I always saw in my mind in. Lisa, thank you for all your patience and kindness. To inspire hope in someone is a great gift, and I thank you for saying, "This rocks!" when I was unsure, and for understanding this story from the very first draft.

I also want to acknowledge The Montclair Writing Group (Tuesday Novelist) whose kind members were always encouraging, generous, kind, and tremendously helpful.

I'd like to extend a final, special thank you to Anna Marie Scillia and Jennifer Casey, who were willing to read all my strange ramblings and help me along.

A final note: suicide affects 41,000 people a year according to the National Institute of Mental Health. If you or someone you know is struggling, please know that there is help and there is always hope. **1-800-273-TALK (8255),** available 24 hours a day, 7 days a week.